THE

FALCONER

THE

FALCONER

ELAINE CLARK McCARTHY

RANDOM HOUSE   NEW YORK

Library of Congress Cataloging-in-Publication Data
McCarthy, Elaine Clark.
The falconer / Elaine Clark McCarthy.
p.   cm.
ISBN 0-679-44874-8
I. Title.
PS3563.C3372F35 1996
813'.54—dc20   95-46296

Printed in the United States of America on acid-free paper.
2   3   4   5   6   7   8   9
First Edition

Book design by Lilly Langotsky

FOR MY FAVORITE AUNT,
RUTH KING BUCHMAN,
ENGLISH TEACHER, SURVIVOR,
INSPIRATION.

ACKNOWLEDGMENTS

To be true to my belief that nothing is wasted, I would have to acknowledge literally thousands of people who have enriched my life. How can I select the few whose help and encouragement have been most valuable to the present effort? Yet I must.

So here are my heartfelt thanks:

To my first readers: Antoinette Czerwinski, Catherine Maclay, F. Jo Mohrbach, and Linda Wroth (aka The Ladies Who Lunch), Carolyn Farrington (fellow writer and confidante since we were both twelve), Cathy Westfall, Kay Cornelius, Ellen Leanse, Lisa Sheretz, Susan Myer, Judy Gertz, and Beth August.

To my agent, Sandy Dijkstra, and her wonderful staff, who made the sale such an exhilarating experience, and to my editor, Kate Medina, whose enthusiasm and insightful comments helped me through the final push.

ACKNOWLEDGMENTS

To Stuart Rossell for introducing me to falconry, and to falconer Bill Murphy, who generously shared his expertise and let me photograph his birds. Needless to say, any falconry mistakes in the text stem from my own ignorance, while whatever I got right I owe to Rossell and Murphy.

Above all, love and gratitude to my husband, Brian McCarthy, for giving me the time and space to write this; to my daughter, Allegra Thayer, who listened tirelessly and cheered me on, and to my son, Stuart Carroll, who always knew I could.

THE
FALCONER

MIDNIGHT OIL

*D*o I remember that first sight of him clearly now, after all that has been? I should have been struck speechless. I should have swooned. Instead, I walked toward him quite calmly, or I thought I was calm. Yet I do remember wondering if I had combed my hair that morning. I do remember being glad I had worn a bra and wishing it were not so plain and businesslike. And I remember thinking of one more thing to add to my "before I die" list—not the list I'd written out, of things a person can actually arrange on purpose, but the mental list of things I would most likely die without: passion. It is a measure of how dazzled I was that I completely failed to see any significance in such a thought at that particular moment.

Why? He looked fierce and remote, a little unreal in a way I couldn't fathom. It wasn't his physical self that seemed not of this world; one of my chaotic thoughts

stood out quite clearly: Here is a man made of flesh. Nor was it that he behaved strangely. He smiled a proper social smile, twin to the one on my own face.

I said something prosaic, "I've come to see your hawks." And he said, "They're in the truck." As if he already knew who I was, had been expecting me. His voice was strong, quiet. I remember his sleeves were rolled back and I could see the veins in his forearms, the beat of his blood. I felt a little dizzy, and wondered if it was a new symptom of my illness, but it passed.

He told me later that his mouth had been dry, that he could hear the blood pounding in his ears. I believed him when he said it, but now I wonder. Could we really have recognized each other with a single glance? Maybe it was only the beauty of the morning, the absence of other people, our acute aloneness, that made us feel the moment to be different, made us see each other so clearly. We must have added the rest in retrospect. His cottony mouth, my sense of falling skyward, outward, opening up.

My head is full of mental snapshots, a memory album. I never owned a camera, but if I had, how different the picture collection would have been. Instead of family groupings, I have a close-up vision of a leaf I held as a small child, brown and curling, with more curl on the left than on the right. Instead of wedding pictures between red plush covers, I see a glass of lemonade on my mother's kitchen table at the old house, half empty, with a fly on the rim. Instead of graduation, there's my mother's face as the cancer killed her, her flesh so shrunken that she looked like a small fierce bird.

And now there's Rhodri, as I walk toward him in the October sunshine, with the edge of a redwood tree's shade just touching his shoulder. So clear that I could this instant count the shadows that lie like tiny fingers on his khaki shirt. Count the threads of the fabric. Count the smile lines at the corners of his eyes, the number of times the bird in the redwood above us cried out, the number of times my heart thudded as he walked toward me. Oh yes, I do remember, I remember it all.

THE BETRAYER

The young doctor who told India about her cancer looked her right in the eye as he did it. He seemed to think he could brace her with his own firmness, but his gaze bounced off her in-turned look as she absorbed the blow. He kept his eyes fixed on her face and gave it to her all at once. Inoperable. Six months at the most. I'm sorry.

"Yes," she said. "I see."

See what? he almost asked. Her eyes looked as if she were staring into the next world already. After she left he broke a rule and had a small, just a tiny, nip of the medicinal brandy kept in the corner cabinet.

Emerging from his office, she stopped outside the door to slip her sweater on over her sleeveless blouse. She saw how the hazy autumn light shed its glory on the pot-holed street, so that the row of old pickup trucks in front of the hardware store, the dog lying on the apron of the gas station, even the raccoon-ravaged trash can on the sidewalk in front of Murphy's Feed and Seed, blazed forth their beingness, and she was pierced with a strange sensation that tightened her throat. Love. She set her jaw and started up the street to where she'd left the old jeep, in front of the grocery store.

I am walking along quite normally, she thought. I am putting one foot in front of the other, and no one observing me will notice that I'm different.

In the blacked-out window of the dentist's office she caught sight of her reflection. No change at all; she had seen that same face half an hour before, on her way down to the doctor's office, unsuspecting. An ordinary woman, not too pretty, not too plain. Khaki pants, a white shirt, a beige sweater, her straw-colored hair pulled away from her face, no makeup, just her lean and sun-scorched self. She stopped and looked more closely at this body she had lived in so comfortably, now the betrayer. There was a saying she had heard: "By the time you're forty you have the face you deserve." She was only thirty-seven; she would have to try to deserve this face a little early.

She stared for a long time, as if she needed to memorize her own features, the cocked wing of each eyebrow that gave her a perpetual look of startled attention, the way her high-bridged nose finished in a point, the embarrassingly sensuous mouth with its lack of a philtrum notch in the upper lip. Of all this, what had she created herself? The faint crease between her brows, a frown mark not from bad temper but from years of forgetting to wear sunglasses. Smile lines at the corners of her

mouth that could mean either a cheerful attitude or something more sardonic. Ambiguous signs, but there was nothing else; the rest, even the leanness, had been given, brought about by forces beyond her reach. Like her whole life.

The bell of the First Baptist Church rang twelve, and doors all down Main Street sprang open; people popped out like cuckoos from a clock, hurrying off to lunch. Across the street, Jean Jones locked up the library and waved.

"Going to eat?"

India shook her head.

"Come on; you're too thin. Besides, I could use some company." Jean crossed the dusty street and took India's arm. "You look poleaxed; something wrong?"

"No, I'm all right," she lied automatically. If she told anybody, it would be Jean, but she wasn't ready yet.

"You're sure? I saw you come out of the doc's."

"Just my annual." They turned into Carly's Cosy Nook and grabbed a corner booth. The smell of frying onions made India feel a little sick.

"I thought you had that a month ago."

"Jean! Change the subject!"

"All right, all right! What are you going to have?"

India looked at the menu, encased in plastic, the leatherette edges frayed with use. Five kinds of burger, eight ways to fix eggs, Club Sandwich, and Tuna Melt. Sandwiches come with Fries, Potato Salad, or Dirty Rice. It all looked the same, same, same as it had always looked.

She didn't see a thing she thought she could put in her mouth. "Maybe I'll skip it."

Jean frowned and opened her mouth, then closed it, turned her eyes back to her menu and didn't look up again until Carly came along with her order book. "Hey, there, Jean. India." There was a subtle difference in the way she said their names, as if Jean were a buddy, India an unknown quantity. India had never wondered about this, though it was Carly's usual way of greeting them. Now, trying to figure out why she had been so oblivious, she missed Jean's order and the pause that should have cued her to give her own.

"Sorry, sorry! Just coffee." She forced herself into the moment, and while they waited for Jean's lunch, India babbled. She talked about the weather, warm for October, usually by this time there's a frost. She talked about the row of sugar pines she was planting behind the house. She talked about the butcher's new truck. Anything. Jean listened and watched, and India could hear her wondering what was up.

Finally the food and coffee came. Jean tucked into her Blue Plate meatloaf while India watched. Sunlight through the window beside them gleamed on the plate; if she blurred her vision a little, she could see rainbows on the gravy. "Is it an unusually beautiful day, or is it me?"

Jean gave her another narrow glance. "What kind of question is that? You're acting very odd."

"Do you ever wonder about the way things look? About what we see and what we miss? Is it the way we're

looking? Or is it . . . never mind." She could see Jean wasn't following her line of thought; she wasn't sure she was following it herself.

"What's going on, India? What is it?"

"It's like there are signals. A pattern that wants to be noticed. I know it sounds crazy." India laughed, wondering if she sounded as out of control as she felt, and everyone in the place glanced at her, mostly trying to do it unnoticed. "Don't mind me. I've got to get outside." She put down a dollar for her coffee and dashed. Jean might think she was off her rocker, but it was Jean's unique talent to think that without making it a judgment.

She walked around town, fascinated by how different everything suddenly looked. How golden, how clear. The post office an epiphany, the fragrance from the bakery an almost unbearable pleasure. Only when, turning the bend where Main Street changed into the road to Arbuckle, she saw the Baptist Church, did she halt in confusion. Beyond it, but invisible from her vantage point, lay the old graveyard. She quickly moved toward it; she would not shirk even this.

Earthquakes and torrential rains had tipped some of the stones to drunken angles. Her parents' stone still stood upright: Leonora Blake, 1916–1979. Roland Blake, 1899–1960. A few places farther back lay Grandmother India Fairweather, Beloved Wife, and her quiet husband, Jonathan. "Father never spoke a word," India's mother had said time after time, as her mind wandered and complaint became her only mode of speech. Poor mother,

India's daughter, then a different India's mother, born to be a butterfly but doomed to live a fragile, pretty cuckoo in an eagle's nest. All turned to dust.

In the farthest corner, Hiram and Beatrice Jenkins, Together In God, missionaries retired to the mountain air for the sake of Hiram's lungs. Great-grandmother had dressed in black every day of her life and managed what no other woman of her line since had ever come close to: the forming of her daughter into another edition of herself, India the First, taciturn, correct, a woman made of stone. Let them lie. The graveyard had always opened in India a kind of wondering sympathy for her mother. It was the only thing that could.

Now she saw for the first time that there was room left, a space beside her mother's grave where someone else might finally rest. Deliberately she sat exactly there, turning away from the stones and looking outward; the dead had the best view in town, down the valley to the west. On a fine morning you could see a hundred miles, but now the sun was shining right into India's eyes; that was why they watered so.

TWILIGHT

I can see my husband Dougie's head against the dying daylight square of the bedroom window. His profile. What is that vertical line right down the middle? Ah: the clear tube of the IV that drips painkiller into my arm. His craggy jaw was once his most outstanding feature; now it's his eyebrows, grown bushy already though he's barely into his forties. They give his face the look of a startled owl. Why did I marry him? Why did I stay? Too late to think about that. I have more urgent questions now.

He hasn't spoken; there was never much to say. I know the time running through his head is counting toward the day, maybe the hour, the minute, when he can be with his girlfriend openly. Poor Dougie. It's funny, really, that this shell, this husk of me upon a bed, can tie him here like a lover: my stringy hair, sunken blotchy cheeks, bones draped in skin. They won't let me have a mirror, but I know; Mother was my mirror, years ago. It's different when it's yourself. Not as bad, in some ways. Not what I thought.

I felt for a moment as I woke today that it was Rhodri's body, not mine, lying on this bed. I grasped my own shoulder, but it was his flesh I felt under my hand, solid and warm. Was he thinking about me then? I know he was, just as he's in my mind each minute, sometimes a hair's breadth below the surface, yet always there. I don't even have to close my eyes to see him, throwing a hawk into the sky, and my body tenses with love and loss. Sometimes I can't tell which is real and which a vision: Rhodri with his wide-winged bird, or my fast-dwindling remains trapped in this bed.

I had it almost figured out, just as I faded into sleep last time. What it all meant. Why I found the falconer too late. Something to do with God, I think. Or gods, the old ones, who liked a good laugh. Taking their ease on Olympus, lifting their cups of foaming nectar and meddling in our lives for sport.

It's these awful drugs: they blur my mind, fill it with irrelevancies when I want to concentrate. So little time left, and no answer yet. There has to be a clue, somewhere, encrypted in the shapes of things: the streaks of jet vapor white across the sky; the mocking dance the flames do in a fireplace at night; the way the falcons' wings turn up at the tips as they glide. A tendency toward the sky. Is that it?

The night is coming. I must think. What if I slide my

punctured arm under the covers, pinch the tube and stop the flow of drugs, hide it beneath my elbow where they won't notice? How soft and slack the skin; it feels a hundred years old. There; now let the mind grow clear as night draws in. Dougie didn't notice, hasn't stirred; was that a snore?

FIRST STAR

*I*ndia Blake was plump the whole first half of her life. All through grade school and high school. Not fat. Just an extra thirty pounds, rounding her cheeks, giving her a little second chin, making a bulge above her waistband. Plump and shy. Never a date, never a pajama party. How could she invite anyone to her house? Crazy mother in her bathrobe all day, hair grown greasy on its rollers: Miss Havisham in the California foothills. Her mother sewed; built crazy clothes that India refused to wear. Things she'd seen on TV. Bell-bottoms with rows of flamenco ruffles all down the legs, and Nehru jackets in gray-blue chintz with big pink flowers, to be worn with strings of cheap beads. India longed to fly from that house, up over the mountains to a land far away.

Dougie Davern was four years ahead of her in school, his jaw still firm, his eyebrows thick but not yet bushy. Captain of the football team, Golden Boy, American icon. Their

eyes never met a single time the one year they were both students at White Creek High. Then he was gone. She dreamed. Perhaps she dreamed of him because he was gone. The falconer once said, "You can tell about people by their absences. By the shape of the emptiness they leave behind." The emptiness Dougie left in her fifteen-year-old heart was the shape of an anchor. She thought it would hold her steady, that it meant something firm and strong. She dreamed of finding solace and contentment in his arms.

She had always felt the world calling, drawing her away from the little Sierra-foothill town of her birth. She used to run away from home at every change of season until she was eleven, when her mother found the key to keep her locked in place: grotesque accounts of what would happen to a girlchild on her own. There were terrible half-human men who would cage her and do dark and nameless things. For months after this, India pushed her dresser in front of her bedroom door at night and slept with the light on. Now she wonders where her mother got those nightmare visions; she never saw anything to match them in newspapers or on TV. Somehow this question is even more frightening than the stories themselves.

Despite the horror tales, which she finally taught herself to disbelieve, her yearning to depart grew stronger, more insistent. She made plans. She would go to college in the East, find a career that would take her far away: paleontology, archaeology, the history of art. When she was grown and strong, she would wander.

Meanwhile the clutch of her mother's needs tightened

like claws around her life. Why, she asked again and again, did they call it "inflation" when all it did was shrink the pension India's father had left? They could barely afford to eat. There was no money for the school trip, the summer camp (foolish waste, when they lived at the mountain's knees already); no money for a car or insurance for a teenage driver, let alone college. India could see her mother's glee at having this excuse to keep her near, and smiled through her teeth; she knew that all she had to do was wait.

The long purgatory of high school finally ended. The scholarships were all arranged; she was nearly free. But as she stepped toward the brink, her mother found one final claim. Cancer, the ace of trumps.

For five years India tended her, at first working parttime at the local bakery just to get out of the house each day; in the end not even free enough for that. Five years of barring the door to keep her mother from wandering, drunk, into the street (always money for booze; India never did figure out how she managed it), of listening to tirades of despair, then silence, of cleaning the messes, holding the wasting hand even at the end, unrecognized and unnoticed.

By the time Leonora Blake died, India's dreams were in mothballs, the scholarships long gone. But Dougie Davern was back, meeting her eyes at last. She was so tired. Even though everything else had changed from the days when she had loved him from afar, there was this one dream left.

She married him. She had thinned down, carved to bone by her service and her sacrifice. Gone was the baby fat, the second chin. She was like a marble angel with a

lamp inside; high broad cheekbones and enormous haunt-
ing dark brown eyes that glowed. No more the timid,
apologetic girl, but a woman who had laid out her dead,
whose dreams lay buried in the carapace of stern necessity.

"What are you thinking?" Dougie would ask when
she fell into a reverie about the past. She felt pressured,
pried at. She wanted to shake the dark thoughts off, not
dwell on them, not dig and examine, trying to find words
soft enough to tell it without howling.

"Come on, you can tell me, pet." He urged her often,
seemed hungry for her confidence the more she held it
back, crouching beside her chair as she stared out the window at the dusk. "Come on, it can't be all that awful. Isn't
that what love is, perfect trust?" His voice went all soft and
squishy when he said it, setting her teeth on edge. "It
wouldn't matter what you'd done," he swore, and she had
to laugh at how far his imaginings were from the truth.

Once she relented, spoke to him about her mother's
final weeks, about how alone she'd felt, how at the end of a
day of bedpans, spit-out food, and curses, she would crawl
into her own bed and lie there shaking, trying not to cry.

"You can cry now," he said. "It's safe here. Go ahead."
His eyes gleamed; she saw that he wanted her to weep, that
he was eager for her to be weak and in need of comfort. He
wanted to eat up her pain like candy, himself blameless and
strong. She felt ashamed for thinking such a thought.

Even though she did her best to protect it at the
start, his passion soon wore off, or burned away in her
flame, like the moth-wing stuff it really was. Numbly, she

noted her own indifference; she stayed. She had filled her time, read every travel or history book in the library, gone on private expeditions into the mountains, bringing home rare grasses and seeds and building a garden of native flowers by dint of sheer determination. Transplanting roots they said would die if moved; germinating seed they said would only grow in the wild. She would never again bow down to "can't." She would gather deer droppings to fertilize the meadow plants, would scrape up sods of forest floor to carry back for the delight of her tamed darlings. She was a force of nature, the Earth Mother not all billowing hips and flowing milk, but lean and strict and hardworking: a priestess, a warrior woman, a queen.

She became interested in the lore of the native people, their herbal knowledge, their rituals. The silent, town-bred remnant of the local tribe opened to her stillness, her edge, her cool kindliness, like the kindness of water running over stone. They gave her a name (maybe it was one of their subtle, secret jokes), calling her after the fox's vertebra she'd found in the forest and wore on a silk cord around her neck: Fox Bone Woman.

Sometimes she thought she might be as crazy as all the other women in her family: her namesake grandmother, her giddy dipsomaniac mother in her gaudy robes, even her dour, angry great-grandam glaring in black bombazine from the parlor wall. But even if she was like them, a sprout of the same root, a leaf of the same branch, it made no difference. Still she stood alone.

NIGHT

I can stand the pain. It's white, and seems to turn and turn like a dog before lying down. I stretch my lips at the nurse as she tiptoes in. "I'm awake," I tell her. I can see her expression of concern and lower my eyelids a fraction to look sleepier; am rewarded by hearing what she whispers as she hands Dougie the evening paper.

"Great tragedy." I think at first they are talking about me, that somehow my death has made the evening paper, though it hasn't happened yet. At least I think not.

"Horrible way to go," he agrees, the paper rustling. "Heroic." Can't be me. Not "heroic."

"Who?" I ask, uneasily, though what could be left in the world to make me uneasy, this near eternity myself?

"One of the smoke jumpers," she says. "Rhodri Mac-Neal." She mispronounces his name, saying *Rod-ri* instead of *Rory*. Most people do, unless they know. The newspaper, as usual, has got the details wrong. He's no smoke jumper; he is, he was, a pilot.

For a moment I am tempted to release the IV line and let nepenthe flow. But my annoyance at the story's inaccuracy gives me time to think, collect myself, hold on. This is a different pain, another question, and I have no time.

Then comes the second shock, as news proceeds from brain to heart. How can I bear it? I've been lying here so long, my only gladness knowing that he was out there, somewhere, he and the falcons, still flying. How? A new question to add to "why?" and make the puzzle deeper. Why such grief, when I knew already I would never see him again? Oh, heart! My love. It's too hard; I don't know how to go on.

LAST THINGS

*S*he'd thought, as she wandered the town after her doctor's appointment, about telling Dougie. The doctor had offered to do it, but she had warned him off. She could predict with awful certainty her husband's reaction; this was just the sort of event that kicked Dougie's sense of Destiny into high gear. There would be speeches, tears, another grand repentance, no doubt, and Clarissa, or whoever the current girlfriend turned out to be, would be banished to await the outcome. The more India thought about it, the more impossible it seemed. It could wait; she would be better able to bear his effusions of sincere but superficial grief once her own initial shock had passed.

When Dougie got home that night, he found India still awake, to his embarrassment. She was making some kind of list, and did not seem to notice the pungent remainder of Clarissa's personal scent that clung to him.

"Whew, had to walk all the way around the old Bower place four or five times today. Some young fellow from Santa Barbara; kept me up there for two hours and then took off without even saying he'd call . . ." It was the best he could do on the spur of the moment, but luckily she wasn't paying much attention. He trailed off and dove for the bathroom and a midnight shower. Never thought to question this break in their routine. Poor Dougie lacked even the most vestigial scrap of imagination, taking for granted that his transparent lies had served their purpose well enough, for India never seemed to guess. Proof positive she knew nothing, or else wouldn't she have made a fearful scene? Take that as given. At such moments, India almost loved him for his innocence.

But this night he could have brought Clarissa herself into their bed, giggles and bitten nails and push-up bra and all. India's concentration had never been so complete. So far the tally read: see the ocean; balloon ride; river raft; find a thunder egg. She was surprised at herself. Sitting at the plain pine bedroom desk to plan what she wanted to do before she died, she had expected a flood of desires. But she was only writing down those goals that were still possible to reach. Winning the Boston Marathon was out, not that her need to run until her lungs burst was very strong. She had entertained the idea for a fleeting moment once, seeing the sweaty triumph on the faces of the winners on TV. Likewise, it would be pointless to write "visit Hawaii." A man who attempts to sell insurance and real estate in a community of three thousand cannot af-

ford such luxuries, even for a wife about to die, no matter how many irons are in the fire.

Other things she omitted because, though possible in themselves, they were beyond her power to arrange, but they made up an involuntary mental list: seeing a comet shower, the aurora borealis, the blooming of the century plant. And all those hawks, endlessly hovering over every meadow; she had never seen one stoop, not once. A lean and hungry life they must lead. So much patience, so rarely rewarded.

But hadn't she heard something about falcons once, weeks ago? Jerry at the post office had mentioned a man, "Some foreign fellow living up toward Vreeland, who keeps falcons, hunts with them!" She'd been waiting in line behind Marie Hacker, had to endure her gush and reminiscences of dear Leonora, with whom she'd been in school, until it was Marie's turn at the window.

Marie had evidently asked a question about the overheard matter of falcons, and Jerry was spouting off as he took a box from Godiva off the highest shelf. "I asked Mike Barstead, the game warden, you know; he says it's all aboveboard, regulated just like fishing. You have to have a license; that's the government for you. Got to have a license just to own a hawk. Fact."

His face had changed when he saw India behind Marie, his manner became more formal. "I've got your package out the back. It said to keep in a cool dry place, so I put it under the steps. Coolest place we've got. I even sent George back to your house with it the next day, but you still weren't there." Marie had raised a fuss then, scolding Jerry for putting her chocolates near the ceiling, where the air was warmest.

India wrote it down: fly a falcon. The first thing on the list she had felt really excited about. A perfect place to start.

It hadn't been as easy as she expected. Jerry recalled nothing. "Falcons? I never said anything about falcons! You must of heard it somewhere else." She'd always suspected that the endless stream of gossip and complaint pouring from Jerry's mouth somehow bypassed his brain.

She tried the local vet, who suggested a bird specialist down in Vinton, but a phone call netted no new information. The pet store in Deer Creek was no help either.

Normally, once she'd set her sights on something, she was as single-minded as a tree root pushing up a slab of sidewalk, but now things were different. Time mattered. She'd been about ready to forget the falcons, move on to the next item on her list. "I don't know where else to look," she was saying to Jean Jones as they waited for the butcher to tenderize Jean's Swiss steaks. "Maybe I dreamed it all in the first place; there's no sign of a tame falcon from here to Route Five."

"What's this sudden interest in falcons?" Jean asked.

"Falcons?" the butcher said. Strange to be buying meat from a nineteen-year-old boy with rosy cheeks, whose mother India had known since kindergarten, a stocky, stubborn girl with pink hair ribbons. "You looking for a falcon, Mrs. Davern?" He was the only one in town

who called her that; it always gave her a bemused sense that there was another self standing behind the real India Blake, a sterner, older woman, waiting imperiously for her share of the attention.

"You know one, Plunk?" she asked.

"Sure. There's a guy comes in here every two-three weeks, buys a gross of frozen quail. Asked me if I could ever get any dead chicks for these hawks he keeps. He bought the old Oneida homestead, off the Vreeland Road. Name's Rhodri MacNeal." Plunk had pronounced it right. *Rory.*

He had no phone, of course, but she thought she could find her way, though she hadn't been up there for years. She set out the very next morning, aiming toward the ridge above China Flat, and found the place within an hour, half by cloudy recollection, half by guess. No one was there. The old cabin had been newly roofed, and freshly graveled paths led from a fiberglass-covered carport to rebuilt front steps, and from there to a row of cages, new wood bright against the silvery weathered boards on the uphill side of the house, six separate wooden enclosures big enough to walk into, with a screened-in passageway outside their slatted doors. The smell was sharp, slightly bitter, and clean, almost overpowered by the scent of new wood.

She sat on the front step, chilled by the morning shade, to write a note on the back of a grocery receipt, the only paper she could find in the jeep, spreading it on her knee: Dear Mr. MacNeal. Then she heard a truck, grunting its way up the slope in four-wheel drive. She half rose, feeling like a trespasser, as it came around the last bend into view: a bright red pickup with a homemade camper shell. Whimsical, incongruous: a small brown-shingle house with red-shuttered windows like a Gypsy caravan, and little open skylights on the roof. All for some birds; India smiled in astonished delight as the truck stopped and he emerged. Rhodri MacNeal. The falconer.

THE FALCONER

*P*eople often remarked that Rhodri MacNeal resembled his hawks, with his keen gold-brown eyes, and his narrow, high-bridged nose. He had played with the idea in an idle moment, brushing his rusty-brown hair straight back from his forehead and observing with surprise how much more numerous were the glints of gray than when he had last noticed. With his hair thus, and an imperious frown, he thought he did resemble Morgaine, his female peregrine. But as soon as he let the hair go, it flopped forward, his mouth relaxed, and all resemblance vanished. He might not have thought so if he could have seen his profile, but he rarely did. He was not a man for mirrors.

The new place was shaping well. When he'd left Idaho, his Forest Service coworkers had all wished him good luck and added the usual notes of alarm and gloomy predictions that speed a parting friend. In this case, that prices in California would be sky-high, Rhodri would never be able to afford a house. Plus the people were weird, different. And the forest would be overrun with tourists. He had never seen the name of White Creek before he heard about the job there, so he had doubts about the tourists. Didn't expect the people to be any weirder than those in isolated small towns anywhere. As for the prices, he had a plan for that, one that fit right in with his need for solitude and space. He would buy an old cabin so far off the beaten path the owner had given up on selling it. Get it cheap.

He'd had little chance to check his judgments about the tourists or the local citizens, but the cabin had been easy enough to find. He'd stuck a card up on the wall of the post office, and it had come to him, even more ramshackle and remote than he'd dared to hope, though not quite as inexpensive.

The birds' accommodations had to be built first, of course. After so many moves, he could fling up a row of cages in a couple of days, while the hawks stayed in the truck. Once that was done he had tackled the cabin roof, which had clearly had no attention for decades. Everyone he met (up to now, only the Forest Service fire crew he flew for, the postmaster, and the butcher) told him that it rarely rained until winter hereabouts. He had never lived in such a place, didn't see how such weather could exist. He had visions of eating cold beans out of a can because every pot he owned was busy catching drips. He bought shingles.

In spite of his hurry, it took two full weeks to lay the new roof, because late summer was the fire season and he had to work. In August there were four major blazes, one of them lasting six days. He lost count of how many passes he flew, how many loads of fire retardant he dropped on how many burning hillsides. Cruising above these areas afterward, he tried to count the patches of spearmint green where the chemical had hit, but there were too many and in any case he needed to focus his mind on learning the terrain.

He was forty-four years old, unmarried and un-missed. At Christmas each year he sent a card to his cousin in Aberdeen, and that was that. He hadn't been back to Scotland in twenty years. His family had moved from Inverness to Toronto when he was nine, and his vowels had altered there enough to confuse Canadians and Scots about the same.

He'd been a bit solitary, even as a kid, child of a writer and a fifties ecology radical. He could never picture his mother without a pen behind her ear, a blot of ink on her middle finger and most likely on her nose as well, hurrying through any nonwriting task that had pre-empted her attention. She'd mothered him casually, with a slightly absentminded love.

It was his dad who'd brought him up, tramping around first the Highlands and then the woodlands of Ontario counting Nature's losses. He'd learned to read by locating which boxes to check on endless tallies on his father's clipboard, and by sitting in his father's lap

finding the keys on the typewriter that added up to im-
passioned letters to editors who rarely printed them.
Knew how to pitch a tent before he learned to write,
how to capture and tag a wild bird before he had his first
date. It was always a relief to let the birds go again, a relief and a sorrow, and those nights he often dreamed of
taking wing himself, and in waking life vowed one day
he would.

As he grew older, his mother's bemused affection
became more personal. It was as if she could only relate to
him in the modality of literature; he had to present a
theme, an unexpected metaphor or hidden meaning. He
remembered clearly the sharp, focused look she'd turned
on him when at his eighth birthday party (a picnic in a
sunny glen, beside the River Carron) he'd said to her,
"This is like *Wind in the Willows*."

"How?" she'd asked.

Pinned down, he'd looked for details. "Not the trees.
The stream, I guess. The noise it makes, and the grass
along the bank."

She'd only nodded, a faint smile. He felt he'd ac-
complished something, that she approved. He tried to
repeat the act, but it fell flat. That taste of her attention
had whetted his appetite, though, and he wouldn't give
up. He tried writing stories to show her, but that didn't
work. Brought home botanical specimens, stray animals,
friends. He learned a lot about what she was indifferent
to: news of the world, complaint, his father's work.
Then one day she saw him handling a piece of quartz

he'd been carrying in his pocket for weeks, a squat crystal he'd picked up on one of his father's trips. She asked what it was, and without thinking he told her, "A thing that fits my hand," and demonstrated how his four fingers precisely encircled its girth, how his thumb fitted in the slightly concave blunt end. He saw her look impressed again.

He never found the rule for her brief bursts of interest, but discovered in himself an instinct that often worked. Brought home the friend who was trying to read all of Trollope in one year, the scribbled note in three kinds of handwriting found in the school hallway, the carved peach pit picked up next to a dead fire left by unknown trespassers in the wilderness. Each time he found a new key, they talked, and more and more often he could find a key in talk itself.

"You're a peculiar bird," she said to him once. "You'll do something strange in life." At sixteen that wasn't what he wanted to hear, and he had let it drop. She'd died soon after that, an aneurysm that he pictured shattering her brain, so he never got to ask exactly what strange thing she foresaw in his future. Certainly nothing like the life he'd actually picked.

Two years later, while Rhodri was in his first year of college, his father was killed helping fight a forest fire. Suddenly it all came clear; Rhodri would make his dreams of flying real, and at the same time do battle with the enemy that had taken his father's life. He left McGill and came to the States, joining the Air Force to earn the skills that he would need. Vietnam was no part of his master plan, but his experience there, the hardest sort of flying you could ever do, looked well on his résumé once he'd survived. He'd done it all—helicopters, parachute runs, transport, and now the chemical drops, which he liked best because he flew alone. But the airplanes had never really answered his dream; it wasn't until he found the falcons that he knew what flight was all about.

There had been women, of course. The usual hormonal madness of adolescence muted by shyness and confusion. Several calf-loves and one fairly long and wholly unrequited obsession with a prom queen two years his senior. As he matured, he was puzzled to note that the women he met seemed to fall into three types: ones who wanted to cling and be sheltered; ones who wanted to control and be master; and ones who just wanted sex. He knew there had to be other sorts than that, but he never seemed to find them. It was surprising how many of the sex-loving sort there were; pleasant companions who made no inconvenient demands. It was enough for now. His heart remained asleep.

Turning forty had troubled him. Though unconventional in their careers, his parents had been in other ways very much in tune with their times, and echoes of this fifties Calvinism still had the power to provoke thought. He didn't feel lonely, got on well with the others on the fire crew and enjoyed the time he spent at work. But returning to his aerie was always a re-

lief. The birds were good company; dignified in repose and glorious in flight; sometimes comical as well, when like greedy children they tried to hide their kill with outstretched wings, glaring defiance at him as he approached.

How was it possible to have a life so perfect and yet to feel an emptiness? He tried to chalk it up to the influence of early impressions, vestigial, as pointless as an appendix, but it persisted without regard for his rationalizations.

The house above China Flat was exactly what he'd always wanted. Solitary, sheltered, but from the sleeping loft commanding a view that seemed to go to the earth's edge without a single sign of humanity. Best of all, this came with only a ten-minute drive down to the mile-wide meadows of China Flat, where the birds could be worked, and again, miraculously, no other house in sight.

He liked to fly them early in the day, with the sun just turning the dew to mist. There were days, like this one, when the world seemed to shift modes, reality becoming magic, and every falconer who ever lived looked through his eyes at the bird as she soared and stooped. He had felt as if he might turn and find a king with his company watching from restless mounts; he could almost hear the jingle of the bridles, the crunch of horses' teeth on a stolen mouthful of meadow grass, the snuffling and muttering of dogs as they explored the fragrant earth. The birds flew perfectly, the sun was never in his eyes, he could not take a step wrong.

As he drove back up to the house, he felt his exalta-
tion floating around him like a feather cape. All the more
shock to see at first a scruffy old army jeep blocking the
spot where he normally parked, and next moment a
woman, apparently cloaked in white, rising from his own
front step and emerging from the shadow of the house
into the clear early light. As if out of the past into the
present. It must have been an optical illusion, maybe he
was even hallucinating in his euphoric state, but it
seemed to Rhodri that in the shadows she had been
dressed in mist. In the light her clothes were plain
enough: white jeans and a man's white dress shirt, some
kind of bone on a cord around her neck. He stepped out
of the truck and faced her across the yard.

CIRCLES

I keep coming back to that, the first moment, the proof of magic on that chilly morning when he stepped toward me and changed my life. What was left of my life. I run the moment over and over through my head; it's better than the drugs they give me, it keeps the pain away, it never fails. Surely that means something. If I could run that moment through my head enough, let it circle and circle until it filled me right up, I might even escape somehow, might spin out into infinity and away from the constant irritations of being cared for.

Bad line of thought; the spell is broken and as if she heard it break, here comes that dratted nurse to keep me from building it back up. Clarissa had better look to her laurels; this nurse will edge her out of Dougie's affections. Trays with soup, newspapers, little consoling words. By the gleam of interest in his eye, I can see he's getting far more pleasure out of her nursing than I am.

They whisper, but do not look my way. The evening sky has faded, the awful yard light's glare obscures the night. Shall I whisper too? Tell them it hurts my eyes and ask to have it out? Even now Dougie twitches with impatience when I ask him to turn off his lovely gadget, the floodlights that come on like magic as the day recedes. He never could understand my preference for the natural night; he was as proud as any pioneer, wresting a few acres of garden from the prairie grass. Mine! his wattage cries, claiming the land, the sky, and his rulership. Once he even canceled a tryst with Clarissa, just because he was so furious that I would turn that light out the minute he was gone.

When I was small, I was allowed to have anything I wanted to eat on my birthday. Dessert first. Cold pie for breakfast and hot pie for lunch; on my eighth birthday I ate nothing but pie all day long; five kinds, I can still count them up. Blueberry, cherry, apple, mince, and lemon meringue. So, though it's not my birthday, I hum a little of the birthday song as Dougie leaves his nice hot soup to go turn out the light.

There. Suddenly the top of the window shows one bright star in a sea of inky blue-black, while below I can see the pale remnant of the day lying along the horizon, exhausted. I look for fire glow, Rhodri's pyre, but there's nothing. It must be to the north, up toward . . . China Flat. Seized with a panic, I ask the nurse for the newspaper, demand to be propped up, telling her to hurry. But panic is more than my strength can sustain, and I end in letting her read it to me: about the fire. And as soon as I hear the first paragraph, I am hit with a wash of relief, or drugs. My struggle has released the IV tube, and once again I'm sinking as the narcotic seeps into my brain. I hear the rest through a fog; he wasn't the pilot that morning, he'd gone to assist the jumpers and his chute had failed to open. It doesn't make much sense; he never jumped. I suppose they've got it wrong again and I will never know the truth. I can only hold fast to the knowledge that at least it didn't happen near his house; the cages are not burning; for a drugged moment I forget that without Rhodri the safety of the cages is nothing, or even less than that.

SIX PAIRS OF EYES

*T*he falconer moves without haste, passing back and forth between his truck and a flat area where he lays out his equipment, seemingly oblivious to the tremors India feels each time he comes near her.

He explains as he works. "These are perches for the goshawks; they've been bow-shaped since the Middle Ages." He shows her three heavy-looking metal arches with spikes beneath the flat bases at either end. Takes them out of the back of his truck and sets them aside on the ground.

The birds are perched on two AstroTurf-covered pipes running lengthwise along the inside of the Gypsy cottage/truck bed. India wonders when he will reach in and take one on his hand, expects this each time he leans into the little cabin, is disappointed each time he emerges with no more than another inanimate object.

"They say the design began at Agincourt," he goes

on about the perches, "when the archers stuck their bows into the ground to give the nobles' falcons a place to perch. Now they're made of steel, you see, with this AstroTurf wrapped round the top for the birds to stand on. Not so very authentic, but it's for the good of their feet." The slight burr of his *r*'s, the rounded vowel sounds, give his speech a rough, homely quality. It sounds cosy, should be cosy, but India can feel an answering vibration in her spine, like the slow sleepy rasp of a cat's tongue.

The perches don't look much like bows, being too small and too acutely bent. "Wouldn't the bowstring get in the way?" she asks, summoning her logical faculties back by force. "Those longbows were what won the battle at Agincourt. If I'd been one of the archers, I wouldn't've let them spoil my weapon just to make a perch for someone's pet."

He laughs. "Perhaps you're right; I wasn't there." Then he takes out a hawk, and she loses interest in her quibble. It's about fifteen inches from hooded head to the talons gripping Rhodri MacNeal's leather-gauntleted wrist, its breast a golden-white with dark brown speckles, its wings and tail various shades of gray, in handsome scallops.

"This one is Morgaine," he says. "She's a falcon, which is to say, a female peregrine. The males are called tiercels, from the Latin "tertius," which means "third," because they're about a third smaller. Unusual in the bird kingdom, but it works for them because they share territory during the time it takes to bring the young up. Both parents mind the nest and feed the eyasses, which is what the young are called, and being different sizes, they prey on different creatures. That's how they can share the same territory without competing."

"Very sensible of them." She blushes, because she can't seem to find a thing to say that doesn't sound flat-footed and inane. The bird sits beautifully still in its leather hood, which is prettily decorated with stamped designs of some kind of flower India doesn't recognize. The shape is sinister, like the helmets of the Third Reich.

He holds the bird easily on his left fist. There's a leather thong attached to the gauntlet, and with his right hand he passes its loose end through the metal ring joining the two ends of the jesses. She's proud that she knows this word for the leather straps attached to the hawk's ankles, but can't think of a way to use it in a sentence. "We have special knots," he says, "because we have to do everything one-handed. Right-handed; you always carry a hawk on the left, so even most left-handers do it exactly like this."

"She's beautiful," says India, longing to touch yet fearful of that great hooked beak. She notices that the falconer offers the falcon no caress; the only handling had been when he pushed his wrist against the bird's legs, so that she had to step onto it or fall backward.

He carries the falcon to the cage, removes the hood, sets her on her perch, and unties the jesses from his glove,

explaining all the while. "They're hooded to keep them calm while they're carried about."

India nods, yes, yes. "How do you fly them?" she asks. "Why do they come back to you?" Chides herself for thinking the answer is obvious; they come back to him because he's a force of nature, irresistible.

He moves back and forth, from truck to cages, one trip for each bird, explaining as he goes. "They come back because they're hungry. You have to feed them every single time, feed them on the fist, always. They're sated now; if I tried to fly one she'd just take off, and I might never see her again. No matter how careful you are, you lose one from time to time. It's part of the sport."

She is feeling a bit chilled, standing in the redwood's shade, and moves to a patch of sunlight nearer the cages, nearer the path he takes moving each bird. "Still, it must be infuriating, to lose one."

"Oh, I didn't say I liked it! They're a lot of work to train."

She's angry with herself now; she came to fly a falcon and it isn't going to happen, and instead of paying attention to the birds, rapidly disappearing into their cages, she's mesmerized by the man, can't take her eyes off him, his bare forearms, the way the ruddy gold hairs gleam in the sunlight. She should be attending to his words, finding sensible things to ask. He's explaining the arcana of the falcons' diet, their long history, the differences between the longwing and the shortwing varieties, but she can only watch the falconer himself, listening with her eyes, her mind bedazzled.

Until he says, "The books don't go into the philosophy of the sport, but I think it was more than a hunt. It's some kind of ritual allegory. All the work, and then letting it go, trusting it will come back to you. And in another sense, the struggle to master Nature, to merge with it, to become one with the force of life even in its darker aspect. You throw the bird up and she catches the air under her wings and climbs it like a ladder to heaven. And the moment she pauses, turns . . . it's like the way you're supposed to feel when you pray, but never do. At least I never did."

He's moved all the birds into cages now, pulls off the glove and turns to look at India. She's speechless. He's grabbed her heart and thrown it into the sky. "You're a poet," she says.

He smiles at some thought this provokes. "I'm a falconer," is his reply.

GOOD-BYE WITHOUT LEAVING

*H*e noticed her wedding ring. She saw his eye flick past it and felt a distance between them increasing. She stood frozen, caught by a confusion of impulses: to take it off, to cover it with her other hand, to wish that she had removed it long ago. It has annoyed her daily for years, sliding around on her thin finger, slipping off and losing itself among the pots and pans as she does dishes. But she couldn't very well remove the ring and pocket it right before his eyes. She crossed her arms over her chest, and immediately felt embarrassed. Would he think she was attempting to hide her breasts, of which, indeed, she had become painfully conscious in the morning chill?

"How did you get into falconry?" she asked.

He had seen something on TV, soon after his return from Vietnam. He'd been stationed at Wright-Patterson, training new pilots on the latest Sikorsky helicopters, feeling restless and dissatisfied. Without the stimulus of live ammunition whizzing around his craft, the thrill was gone. He knew he would get no more training that was useful to his long-range goal; he was simply working out his hitch. Then this PBS program came on; he was watching TV to fill an empty evening, and it changed his life. He did the research, wrote, phoned, and when he was discharged he was ready. He took his savings and flew straight to Scotland, for two years lived and worked in the only falconry school in the English-speaking world, and found himself a soul.

"Soul?" she said. "Do you really believe that?"

"I know it. It's right here." He pointed to his solar plexus with a grin. "When I watch the birds I can feel it, something like a heart. Bigger."

She didn't get the grin. "Are you serious?"

"Partly. It's strange, flying. You look down and you see patterns that are only visible from the air. A river wandering across the land, with all its little tributary streams, looks just like the veins in a leaf. The ocean looks like a huge piece of rough silk. Do you ever feel as if things are trying to talk to you?"

"Sometimes." She smiled a little at the irony of it, of him asking if things talked to her and of her reply, so calm, so equivocal, and all the while she struggled to hide her feeling that every atom of his physical self was calling to her: "Closer, come closer." He didn't seem to be aware of it. Maybe if he could look down at the top of his own head he would see rays of energy making a halo all around him, holding her in his magnetic field so that she stayed there talking when it was clearly time to go.

"You'll be thinking I'm some kind of a crackpot."

"Oh no. I've seen it too. The way everything has a shape ..." She felt foolish; of course everything had a shape, what a stupid thing to say.

"Yes," he said.

There was nowhere to take it. They'd been standing too long, he unconsciously picking at a chalky spot on the leather glove, she in her ridiculous arm-folded pose. The sun was higher. She supposed he had work to do. She backed away a step.

"I'm sorry you didn't get to see them working. Maybe you could come back another time, earlier in the day?"

"You wouldn't mind?"

"I'd like to show you. Only I fly them just a little after dawn, about six-thirty. Can you come that early?"

"Oh, yes," she said. "That's not a problem. Shall I meet you here?"

He hesitated a moment, then said yes. Perhaps he was already having second thoughts. She thanked him formally and took her leave. The day seemed to dim a little as she drove away.

RHODRI SAID

*H*e thought at first she was a ghost. They'd told him when he bought the old place that there was one, but gave no details as to age or gender. He knew well that any lonely spot, unlived in for years, would attract such an idea. And what was a ghost, anyway, but another sort of person?

As she came into the sunlight he realized she was not that other sort of person, at least, though what sort she was he could not tell. Certainly not the usual sort. Maybe some kind of cross between a woodsy woman and a barbarian queen.

She walked toward him as if she owned the earth, her large dark eyes seeming to open his face and inquire into his mind. No "hello," no apology for trespassing or parking in his way. Right to the point: "I've come to see your birds." And instead of questioning her—who are

you, how did you find me, and why?—he merely said,
"They're in the truck."

He found it difficult to remember exactly how it
had gone after that. He'd babbled, droning on and on
about the hawks as he caged them, probably boring her
to death. She'd made an intelligent remark about that old
legend of the bowmen at Agincourt inventing the falcon
perch. All these years he'd taken that tale as gospel, and
in seconds she'd demolished it. Of course she was right;
once you doubted the story, its weaknesses suddenly re-
vealed themselves. What self-respecting archer would
shove his weapon into the dirt for some filthy, militarily
useless bird to spoil with its talons? It had come over him
that she would understand anything he said; more, that
she could instantly tell the true from the false, like an
oracle.

Which hardly accounted for the other feelings, the
warm pull of tension in his lower belly, the desire to reach
out and touch that odd upper lip right where the
philtrum ought to be, trace it with one fingertip. To pick
up and examine the piece of bone that hung just between
her breasts.

He saw that she wore a wedding ring, and tried to
abandon those thoughts, but they sprouted legs and ran
after him, refusing to be left behind. He could see them,
shaped like body parts trotting along in his wake. She had
laughed until the tears came when he told her this, later
on. No particular body parts; he hadn't focused his mental image that closely or held it for very long. Just little

flesh-colored potato shapes with arms and legs and tiny bowler hats, running furiously down a dirt road. "Very tasty little thoughts they are, too," she said (later) and demonstrated her theory of what they represented until everything else blurred away.

He'd schooled himself to see her as nothing more than an attractive married woman with a curiosity about the birds. He'd told her everything and she had listened and expressed her interest, and thanked him politely, trying to appear satisfied. How was it possible for her to be satisfied, when she had not seen them fly? He made the offer, half expecting her to turn it down with some excuse: Oh, I have to make breakfast for my family, I could never come that early.

Instead, her tone when she said "that's not a problem" awakened all those thoughts again. It was a tone that said, without shouting it, indeed trying to conceal it, that her husband was another sort of person, too. A foolish sort, if he had made himself so negligible in her life that she could come and go without comment, no matter what the hour. Rhodri felt the tension in his upper abdomen loosen and realized for the first time that he had almost been holding his breath for her answer. And the other tension returned tenfold.

"What's your name?" he asked, following her to her jeep.

"India," she said. "After my grandmother."

"It suits you," he said. He didn't ask for the rest of it. The rest of it was entirely beside the point.

MESSAGES IN SANSKRIT

*S*o that was how we met. Debating the existence of meaning in the early morning sunlight of October, air clear and ripe with the scent of pine, ringing with birdcall. It reminded me of when I was a little girl, opening the screen door after breakfast and being reborn, from dim house into shining day. How each time the world seemed to pick me up and swing me high over its head, like a laughing father full of joy.

If things have meaning, that meeting surely did. It was all there: the bright promise of completion, and the valedictory light of the dying year. Large things within small things; the falcon's power of flight restrained by leather straps with bells. Fourteen years of marriage in a phrase, and death itself in the claw of a half-tamed bird.

And what of me? Death was inside me too, and inside him, as it is within everyone. And yet the sun shone and I, for one, was happy. All the rest is that; how happy I became. Happy. Such a childish word. A small word, for a feeling so immense the sky was barely able to cover it. I thought it was something to leave behind, for Rhodri to recall. Instead he's dead before me, and I'm the only one left with the memory, and barely time enough to play it through again. Heaven in retrospect.

FORWARD

She slept very lightly that night, frequently rousing to check the sky. Yet when the alarm clock gave its preparatory click at five-thirty, she heard it in time to hit the switch before it truly rang, and rose refreshed, and glad to leave Dougie sound asleep. Not that he would wonder where she went; he was too used to her absences, too indifferent.

The first smoky light of dawn was filtering through the treetops; the birds were waking up. Her thoughts about this meeting had come in starts and stops. She caught herself planning an outfit of dark green slacks, snug and flattering, a white silk shirt, her suede jacket. She rejected that idea, deriding the impulse; she might as well show up in a miniskirt and spike heels. Sweats, the other extreme, were unthinkable. What would she wear if she were meeting Jean? If anything, she ended up erring on the side of utility; a pair of pale gray bush pants she often wore on her plant-hunting hikes, a pale gold flannel shirt, a charcoal-gray wool pullover. As she looked at the chosen clothing, laid out on the spare-room bed, she laughed at herself; she had picked the colors of the birds.

Again in the shower, start and stop. She soaped with scented gel, then washed the smell off and later skipped perfume, though she normally wore it. No makeup, that was standard. She did blow-dry her hair, arguing with the critical voice inside her: it would be cold out there. She'd catch her death (that would be ironic) with wet hair. When she was done, the shoulder-length, pale gold-brown mass shone like a halo. She fastened it firmly back as usual, but with her best tortoiseshell clip.

And wondered why she was being so stern with herself. Certainly she had no qualms about Dougie. It had been years since he'd shown any desire to exercise his "conjugal rights." Yet she would not deliberately set out to seduce some stranger, though he warmed her thoughts to the boiling point. Better to turn to drink, like her mother, than to sink so low in her own estimation. She took off the tortoiseshell clip and used instead one of her everyday, cloth-covered elastic bands, a red one.

The miniskirted tart of her imagination followed her out the door and shivered in the early morning chill. India almost felt sorry for her in her skimpy rabbit coat, nothing but stockings to protect the greater part of

those legs. Then she forgot about her as the morning possessed her.

The sun was not yet over the horizon, but near enough that there was light to bring up halftones. The pines a greenish black, the scar of the driveway in between a brownish white. She stopped to listen and heard a vibrant silence, no sound the ear could catch, yet the sense of living things all around. Then a bird chirped in a nearby tree. It would be a pity to shatter that stillness by starting the jeep, but she found herself equal to it.

She had never been through town so early in the morning. No cars, no lights, except in the bakery, where the owner, her part-time boss, toiled to make the town's breakfast bread. India gunned the motor and sped past, then stopped, made an illegal U-turn in front of the bank, and zipped back to tap on the bakery window, begging a couple of new-baked rolls.

Off again, with the rolls under her sweater to keep them, and herself, warm, she regretted the impulse as too familiar. Too accommodating. Too friendly. But she couldn't regret the heat; it was time to put the top on the jeep for the winter; the wind in her face was painfully sharp.

And always there was a thought of him beneath everything else. Incoherent; not a picture, nor a fantasy, nor a desire. He was just there, like someone hiding behind a tree, or standing slightly beyond the edge of her vision.

There were plenty of attractive men in town. Some

you might even say were better looking than Rhodri MacNeal. Men with faces kind, or handsome, or dissolute, bodies ruggedly strong, broad, tall, muscular or fine, and many gone to seed. Deep voices, booming laughs. Plenty who were game for a fling with a married woman. There had never been even a twitch of temptation, never a thought of what might be. Why not?

As she drove up the steep and ill-paved Vreeland road, she grew warmer; sugar pine and Douglas fir provided shelter, and the chill lessened as she slowed, maneuvering around tight curves, gearing down for potholes the size of bathtubs. When she turned up the Oneida road toward Rhodri's house, the pavement ran out entirely and the going became even slower. She wondered how so much impatience could fit inside her finite chest.

She was assailed by doubts as she drew closer. That hesitation after she'd accepted his invitation; he didn't really want her there, was only being polite. He'd seen her ring. Of course any worthwhile man would have some fairly important scruples about making love to a married woman. Realizing what she'd just thought, she groaned aloud and everything she'd been trying to ignore burst plain upon her.

She stopped the jeep, switched off the engine, and sat shaking in the middle of the road. Face it, face it, face it. She didn't want to look. She didn't know why she didn't want to look. Wasn't it the stuff of legend, of song and story? Discontented wife finds solace and fulfillment with handsome stranger? She had always hated those

stories, with their implication that a woman's happiness depended on a man. So tacky. Pathetic opiate for weak females of little imagination and less dignity.

But oh god she wanted him. She wanted his hands to reinvent her skin, she wanted his eyes to find her there behind her face and release her. She wanted her heart thrown into the sky; she wanted to fly. She wanted it before the dark closed in. So much dark, and so soon.

The only trouble was, she didn't know if he could want it too. But he might. Please, whatever god may be, he might.

A SLIVER

OF THE SUN

*R*hodri had promised himself he wouldn't wait for her. The husband might claim her after all, or some other duty, or just the lack of real desire to be there. He wasn't going to stand around like a flightless bird, hoping. The moment the sun edged over the horizon, he'd be gone. It was due at six thirty-two; he'd checked the paper. Three more minutes. Of course, they might measure the time of rising where it was flat; it would take longer to climb over the top of a mountain ridge. Three more minutes and she would be late. After all, she was married.

It was horribly like being a teenager again; the nervousness, the certainty that he would offend her somehow, misread signals, act the fool. He told himself over and over that it couldn't matter. Whatever he might have thought her tone of voice meant, she *was* married, and in these days, with marriage so easy to get out of, what could that mean but that she wanted to stay with her husband? She wasn't

the sort of woman to have a meaningless fling; he felt quite sure of that. So. She was only coming up to look at the birds, she just wanted to see the falcons worked. That was all. A curiosity; a new experience for her. It was enough. Would have to be enough. After all, she was married.

He checked his watch. Six thirty-two. But the sun had not yet put its edge above the mountaintop. Rhodri went into the house and brought out the thermos of coffee, put it on the truck's seat. He checked the birds again, making sure the folding chair he'd added to his usual load wasn't going to slide around in transit and hurt one of them. It would be all right; he had his imagination on a rein again. Morgaine shifted uneasily on her perch and he regretted the cologne he'd put on after the sitz bath. Some kind of water heater was definitely going to have to be next on his list of home improvements.

Six thirty-five. He looked to the east, and there it was, just the tiniest sliver of gold, right at the top of the highest peak. He was definitely going to have to leave without her; his whole body seemed to fill with disappointment. Stupid, she was married.

Then came the sound of her jeep, whining up the last steep grade just out of sight, and his heart rose with a leap, like one of the birds taking flight.

BREAKING FAST

*S*he drew right up beside his truck; better than stopping at a distance and having to walk toward him while he watched. He was smiling, so that for the first time she saw his eyes lit up, the pleasant creases of his face. When she stepped out of the jeep she realized what a peculiar bulge the rolls made under her sweater, and pulled them out. "Breakfast," she said.

"Great. I've got coffee." He reached into the front seat through the truck window and pulled out a large red thermos and then a pair of wide-bottomed cups.

"Aren't you freezing?" she asked. He was wearing only jeans and a yellow-and-black plaid wool shirt, and the sleeves of that were rolled up to the elbow.

"I run hot. Why don't you pour the coffee, and I'll get you something to wear over that sweater."

She held the thermos and watched him as he walked toward his house, the way his back curved into the heavy

shoulders, the way he held himself; a little stiff. He knows I'm watching, she thought, and smiled, and turned and put the cups down on the hood of the truck and poured coffee into them.

When he came back, carrying a Pendleton jacket, a heavier version of his own shirt, she was leaning on the truck, the smile still on her face, her hands around a mug.

"You look pretty pleased with yourself," he said, handing it to her. "Put that on. It'll get warm soon now that the sun's up."

"Thanks." She set her cup on the truck hood and slipped her arms in the jacket, too large for her even over her shirt and bulky sweater. The sleeves hung down inches beyond her fingertips and she stood there looking at them and laughed, feeling about fifteen.

He grinned and took one sleeve himself and turned it back, and it scared her, how much she yearned for him to just lean down and kiss her. She pulled back, turned up the other sleeve herself.

"Time to get going," he said, acting as if he hadn't noticed, but he was silent as they climbed into the truck.

"Do you have to fly them this early?" she asked quickly, knowing better than to let the silence grow pronounced.

"Doesn't matter, as long as you do it at the same time every day. I picked dawn because I'm finished in time to go to work, days I'm on."

"What do you do?"

"Fly for the Forest Service. Drop chemicals on forest fires. Search and rescue. Whatever they want. You?"

She shook her head. "Nobody ever asked me that before. I'll have to think about it." She handed him a roll and bit into her own, a good excuse not to talk.

He dropped into a low gear to ease them down the same impossible road she'd just come up. What do you do? Such a simple-sounding question, like "who are you?"—with no answer that could encompass the truth. Between sips of coffee and bites of bread she did her best; she told him about the bakery, how she'd progressed from counter work to decorating cakes, but it was only occasional work in such a small town. About the garden, the illegally transplanted California poppies, the lupine and the sage, the unidentifiable plant that grew just at the snow line, with flowers so small you could hardly see them. About her friends from the tribe, the herbal baths they took for certain ills, the things the old women knew. She laughed. "I sound like some kind of crazy medicine woman, brewing potions, gathering strange stuff in the moonlight, conning secrets out of the elders of the tribe."

"You ought to write the secrets down," he told her. "People would be interested. Don't let it get lost."

"I should," she agreed, knowing there was too little time left. "So much gets lost."

When they arrived at China Flat he showed her how to set up. Brisk and businesslike, he handed her the three bow perches and indicated the line where she should anchor them, just so far apart. He planted three others himself in a line parallel to hers, perches made of a block of wood atop a metal post, also covered with As-

troTurf. Hooding each bird for the thirty-foot walk, he moved them from the truck to the perches, tied them and took the hoods off. Then he got out the folding chair and placed it where she could watch, farther into the meadow and to one side, well out of the way. She stuck her hands under the front of the jacket for warmth, and sat.

The first bird leapt from the perch onto Rhodri's fist when he went to pick her up. It was the peregrine he called Morgaine, one of the three longwings. Once more he dropped the little hood over her head, tightening it by pulling two strips of leather at the back, one with his free hand and one with his teeth. He'd slipped back into the lecture mode of their first meeting, telling her how the longwings were used only to hunt flying prey. The short-wings, which, unlike the longwings, were aerodynami-cally equipped with braking power, were used to hunt ground prey: rabbits, for preference.

"You have to weigh her first," he explained as he nudged Morgaine onto a scale with a perch. "Each bird has a flying weight; if she's too heavy, even by an ounce, she might not be hungry enough to come back. She's one pound, fourteen ounces today; that's all right."

He carried the bird twenty feet or so into the meadow beyond the perches and, slipping her hood off, he held her high. She seemed to rise on tiptoe and ex-pelled a dropping. "We call that muting; they usually do it before they take off. Makes them that much lighter."

He raised his arm a bit, almost tossing her into the air. India watched the bird's rapid rise, each beat of her mighty wings thrusting her higher. She reached an altitude of perhaps forty feet and turned to glide back toward Rhodri, dipping down, then rising again in a movement like flirtation.

"She'll cruise around a little, warming up; we'll just let her do that for a few minutes." India watched; the falcon never went far, always turning and seeming to accelerate as she flew back toward him.

Rhodri was getting something out of his supply box: a string with a couple of robin-size gray wings tied together at one end.

"This is the lure; now watch." He stepped out to where he'd released the falcon, gave a long sharp whistle, and swung the lure around and around his head. Morgaine turned, seeming to see it even before her head came around. She bore down on it like a winged express train, at the last moment thrusting her legs forward, so that Rhodri's sudden yank was barely in time to snap the lure from between her outstretched talons.

"Did you see? They kill with their talons, not their beaks. Grab and twist. The beak's just for eating; it's the knife and fork." He swung the lure again, again yanked it out of the falcon's grasp just as it seemed she could not fail to seize it. India was sitting forward on the chair, holding her breath. It was so beautiful.

"Now we'll see about your nerve, shall we? I'll fly her

right over your head. Did you notice how she drops down below the lure and then rises to take it from below? She'll be coming right at you."

He moved behind India and she heard the string hum as he swung the lure in the air. Morgaine saw it and swooped down nearly to the ground, no more than fifteen feet in front of India. Then the hawk rose to the bait, and India saw her glowing golden eyes coming almost straight toward her, felt the breeze of her wings as she soared inches above her head, and laughed out loud in absolute delight.

A LURE

*I*t was the laugh that did it. All the changes of the morning vanished like mist and he barely jerked the lure out of Morgaine's reach in time, had to summon all his strength to walk forward into India's sight at just this moment. He'd been in turn nervous, impatient, excited, wounded, soothed, interested, impressed; his emotions bobbing up and down like a cork on the ocean. No more; it was all solidified into an iron determination to have and hold this woman, married or not.

"That was great!" she was saying. "It was . . . it was . . ." Her face was radiant; he'd never seen anything so glorious in all his life.

"Want to try it?"

"Can I?" She jumped to her feet, her eagerness visible in every line of her body. She was so alive. He could feel her vitality like an electric field, was sure his hair was standing on end.

"Sure, it's not hard." He brought her the lure; she met him halfway. He had to be very careful their hands didn't touch as he passed it to her; the spark would surely short-circuit every nerve in his body. "Just swing it around your head, and when she's getting close, give it a yank." He stepped back and watched, feeling her pleasure, her concentration as she looked around first to see where the hawk was, then carefully arranged the string, checked the hawk again, and waited to start her swing until the bird was at a distance and turning toward her.

"She sees it!"

"That's it, just keep it up there . . ." Again the falcon stooped near the ground and rose to take the lure. "Now!"

His coaching was unnecessary; just as the powerful talons were stretched forward to clutch, India jerked the lure sideways and down, laughing with delight.

"Perfect. Like you were born to it."

"Don't they get cross?"

"They're very persistent. Go ahead; have another go."

She threw the lure three or four more times while Rhodri watched. "It's like teasing death," she said, "or . . . you know those nature programs, sometimes they'll show a litter of some kind of cubs; fox or wolf or lion? When I watch those, I always wish I could be one of the cubs and play too. It's like that."

She seemed to grow sad, looped the line of the lure and handed it back to him.

"I'll bring her in, this time," he said. "You watch, then you can do it with the next bird."

He fetched a skinned quail out of the cooler, explaining, "They like quail better than what's on the lure."
Concealing the food in his fist, he tossed the lure up again
and swung it in its circles, and this time when Morgaine
reached for it with those inch-long talons it was there.
Immediately she dropped to the ground with it, and Rhodri pulled her toward him by reeling in the lure. He made
a clicking sound with tongue and teeth, showed her the
meat. She abandoned the lure and jumped onto his wrist.
Letting only a bit of the meat show, he quickly did his
one-hand knotting trick to fasten her to the gauntlet by
her jesses, then let her pull the meat up where she could
eat it. She tore into it, ripping gobbets off its little carcass,
crunching the bones with her beak. In less than a minute
she'd consumed it all. "Nothing to it," he said. "Your turn
now. Take Sir Kay; she's always next."

"Funny name for a female; wasn't Sir Kay one of
Arthur's knights?"

"Hawks are like boats; they're all called 'she', no matter what the actual sex."

He put Morgaine back on her perch and handed the
glove to India. She pulled it over her left hand eagerly, no
flinching away from the smear of quail guts near the fist.
She quietly approached the bird and pressed her wrist
just above its feet. Sir Kay balked, would not get on,
wings flapping wildly as she tried to keep her balance
against India's push. India didn't give up, and finally,
grumpily, the bird complied. "I'm not too sure about this
knot," she said.

"Pull the tail out of the last loop," he instructed. "Now all you have to do is pull on it and the rest will unravel. Be sure you've got a good grip on the jesses first."

"I get it." She threaded the jesses between the gauntlet's fingers just as she'd seen him do, untied the tether and without further question tied the same knot to fasten Sir Kay to the glove. When she rose and turned toward him, her face shone with pride and pleasure. He wished he had a camera, but it didn't matter; he would remember that moment for the rest of his life.

SMALL HOURS

I don't feel tired. Why would I? Lying in this bed for so long now, it's a miracle I can sleep at all. Drugs. Dougie still there in his chair, he's doing his "duty," I should have expected no less. Poor Dougie. I wonder why *he* stayed? And how appalling of me never to have questioned that before. I certainly didn't give him much to stick around for. Maybe he was afraid of what his dad would say, an awful man who liked me. One more thing I never understood. One among many.

Frank said once, "Dougie wishes he were an Eskimo, so he could put me out on the ice." Right to Dougie's face. He meant it to wound, and I could see it did, though Dougie just laughed. Said something about holding with those who favored fire, and looked superior. He liked to show off the bits he remembered from college, especially at moments such at this. It was clear from Frank's expression that he had never heard

the phrase, probably never even heard of Robert Frost, and didn't know what Dougie meant. One of those guys who sends his kid to college and then can't deal with it when he comes back better educated than his old man. He looked bewildered, just for a split second, and I felt sorry for him, though I never could keep that up for long.

So I said, I was so proud of this, I said, "I would have taken you for more of an ice man, myself, Dougie," and I turned to Frank and recited the whole poem so he'd know. Emphasizing the relevant parts, especially the bit about ice being like hate. Dougie was so astonished at hearing me quote Frost in his father's knotty-pine paneled rec room that he missed the insult, but Frank got it. He smiled at his son, and Dougie shut up, unable to figure out how he'd ended up losing that round. What a sorry little scene.

Still, I suppose living is the best revenge; whether well or not doesn't really matter. And he will live, will move Clarissa into the house as soon as he decently can, unless he decides he prefers the nurse. They'll make love in this very room. Maybe even be happy here. I hope they will. It's been empty so long, with an emptiness the shape of me. When I die, the air will come back into the room, that I've filled with my absence. Why? My friends seemed present enough. Reba Carson at the bakery with Earl, nothing but flour and sugar in their conversation all day long, but how she laughed, even when something went wrong. The time she dropped a tray of bagels onto the chocolate-frosted cake for Jimmy Davenport's eleventh birthday and invented chocolate-frosted bagels. Laughed until she was beet red and I thought she'd burst a blood vessel.

Damn these drugs; my mind wanders. Though of course these things too are shapes. Laughter, scorn, wandering itself, even a chocolate bagel might mean something. I brought a couple to the falconer once; he didn't like them much. Didn't care for sweets, but loved a salted nut; he said it as he licked a drop of sweat out of that little hollow at the base of my throat, after an afternoon in bed. A salted nut. We'd been laughing and I was weak and tired and still filled with something light, like helium. It was toward the end, when the cancer's insidious foreclosure proceedings were getting too insistent to ignore. Now it owns the house, and I'm about to be evicted. A soul on the street. Or not.

One time Rhodri asked, "Do you believe in angels?" I had never given it much thought. He said, "I think we leap from our discarded bodies like a falcon off the fist, spread our new wings and just take off." That would be nice, to have wings, to play with the falcons without having to keep them hooded, without having to tie those one-handed knots.

CLAIMING FREEDOM

"It's not your fault," Rhodri said, as they rode up toward his house, only five birds in the back of the truck. "You did everything right. You expect to lose about thirty percent of your birds; I've lost half a dozen myself, over the years. It's not your fault."

India was too close to tears to speak. That lovely creature, leaping from her wrist and rising into the sky. It turned and swooped back overhead, then tilted right and rose and rose and rose. Behind her, Rhodri had started to whistle, a loud, shrill sound that would probably carry for miles in the cold morning air, but seemed, for all the response it got, not to be reaching the departing bird at all. "Damn," he had finally said. India stood watching until the bird was lost to sight, her throat closing with disappointment.

"Come on," he urged, steering the truck around the largest pothole. "Don't take it so hard. She'll probably be back tomorrow or the next day. I've been training them on that spot for weeks, ever since they finished their moult; she'll know where to come when she gets hungry."

"Do you think so?"

"Half of them do. Don't worry about it. It wasn't your fault."

She laughed, a little shakily. "She probably did it just to discourage me."

"She's always been an ornery one." "Ornery" sounded strange in his muted Scots accent, a lot more *r* than most Californians would use. His exotic vowels soothed her; there was magic in being from somewhere else.

"How far do you think she'll go?"

"No telling. She has no territory of her own, here, so she'll live up to her species' name and wander a bit. Some falconers attach a small radio transmitter before they fly a bird, so that if it takes off they can track it. Much good that does; waste of time in my book. Short of ruining good longbows for perches, I like to do things the old way."

"You should come and talk to Josephine Red Smoke some time. She'd like you. She'd like the hawks. She might not think much of the cages, though."

"I don't think so much of them myself, but without them you're just another birdwatcher. The cage is the price I pay to be a falconer."

She thought some about prices. "It helps to know what you're buying."

"Aye, it does that."

They seemed to arrive back in no time at all. He pulled the truck under the port and shut it off, but didn't get out. Turned to look at her. She was facing forward, but felt his eyes on her profile. "You're a bit hawklike yourself," he said. "That high-bridged Roman nose, like mine. There's Destiny in some shapes. You should take up the sport." She turned to look at him then; he seemed to have read her mind.

"How long would it take? To learn it, I mean. To get one of my own and train it?"

"It's the right time of year to start. You can't do anything in the summertime because of the moult, but by fall that's over and the game season starts. You could begin now, learn a lot in the next few months. You have to serve a two-year apprenticeship before you're allowed to own one yourself."

"Too long," she said, unsure how much to tell him. A new fear occurred to her: that he might be patient. Careful. Testing the water with each step, waiting for signs, thinking there was time. If she hinted that her days were numbered, would he be put off? Or was he disinterested in the first place? And if he did have some feeling for her, even the smallest beginning of a feeling, surely she should warn him. It was all so slippery, impossible to grasp. She shivered.

"I'm keeping you out here in the cold. Come inside and I'll make a fire." The day begun with such a bright promise of sun had turned cloudy, dark.

"I am a bit chilled," she argued aloud and to herself. She could go in without looking as if she was looking.

Why all this shyness and hanging back? The image of that miniskirted, desperate floozy self leapt to her mind's eye for an answer. Horrible if he looked at her and saw that. She climbed out of the truck.

"I'll just build a fire and then put the birds away." He led the way down the gravel path, opened the door and turned to look at her, standing back. "It isn't much," he said. "Bachelor digs. Don't be shocked." Stepping past him, she peered into the dim house, her eyes taking a moment to adjust; then she crossed the threshold.

There was only one room; a deep armchair at the far end, a kitchen table with two straight chairs nearer by, close to the cookstove and sink. Another table against the same wall at the room's dark farther end. The bed was above that end of the space, in a loft. She looked for a light switch, then laughed at herself. There were no wires going to this place, so far from town. A kerosene lantern, two kerosene lamps, and a state-of-the-art, freestanding, fuel-efficient fireplace, located beneath the sleeping loft with its chimney-pipe angled out the back. Pale silver light entered through windows on three sides; she could hear from the loft the ticking of a clock.

He stepped in after her and shut the door, and even with her face turned the other way she could feel herself blushing bright enough to light the whole place. She half expected that the next thing would be his hands on her shoulders, but he stepped around her, went to the fireplace, and stirred with a poker among the embers of an earlier fire, throwing in more wood from a pile nearby. It blazed up quickly. "Sit here." He drew the armchair nearer the warmth. "I'll be right back."

He was out the door again before she could move, leaving her to look around. But there was little to see, and she was tired from her early morning, the excitement and the sorrow; she sat in the armchair and leaned her head back. And fell asleep.

SPLITTING WOOD

AND HAIRS

*R*hodri put the birds away quickly, on automatic pilot. He cursed to himself as he passed Sir Kay's cage with Morgaine, last to go in. Stupid bird, to go off like that just when India was enjoying herself so much. She was a difficult woman to read; one moment laughing like a child, the next sad and remote, or again suddenly impressive, like a falcon with its wings spread, about to take wing. Hard to follow her lead. Yet she hadn't said or done anything that definitely meant "no trespassing." And he had caught one look, that moment when she turned toward him after he'd said she looked like a hawk, a look that for just a moment seemed to pierce him to the bone.

He gathered more wood and returned to the house, and there she was in the armchair, curled up asleep. Lightly, it seemed, for she roused when he put down the wood, though he did it as quietly as he could. "Coffee?"

"I'd better. I don't want to nod off driving back."

"Not much chance of that in this weather. It looks like it might snow."

If it did, she would be caught here. He wished for the first time that he had a phone, a radio, some means for her to call out, so that no search party would appear if she failed to come home. Foolish thought.

"Not likely," she said, and it took Rhodri a second to remember they'd been discussing snow. "We're only at about three thousand feet; not high enough to get snow very often, and it's too early in the year for rain."

Rhodri was scooping coffee into the filter. "Can I help?" she asked.

"Nothing to do; just relax. Stay near the fire; keep warm. You'll need a good toasting before you try to go anywhere in that open jeep." He brought the kettle to the woodstove and put it on, set cups and the coffee pot and coffee in its filter on the little table nearby, then lifted one of the kitchen chairs to straddle and look at her. "You can see I don't get much company, or I'd be better equipped."

"You keep it nice and clean."

He felt a guilty grin forcing its way onto his face. "I did a bit of tidying last night. Just in case."

"Did you indeed?" She smiled back, a smile that looked like relief. "I like the way it smells; pine needles and new shingles and . . ." she paused and sniffed, "earth. It smells real."

Some kind of tension had gone out of her; she lay back in the armchair relaxed, a woman in no hurry. Yet she kept her gaze on him, not a daunting stare, but moving as he moved, listening with her eyes, meeting his hungry look fearlessly and with no defense. Some Rubicon had just been crossed. "Why" was always a mystery, and never more than now. He thought of the ancient Elusinians, who celebrated the unknown in their worship, and understood the impulse to give thanks for things concealed from sight.

SURPRISE PARTY

I don't know how we managed it, that strange transition from fear and doubt to confidence. It was more than just knowing he'd put his house in order on the chance I might come in. Maybe it was the fact that I'd slept the moment I arrived there, at the heart of his domain. I always found it difficult to sleep in strange places, difficult to sleep next to Dougie all those years. And when I opened my eyes, there he was, putting logs into a log box with the most exquisite care, as if they were made of china and might break. I felt so much at home. The firelight made his skin seem red-gold, and the warmth of it was creeping out into the room so that my icy toes began to thaw, and everything was perfect as it was, the best of all possible worlds come round at last.

It wasn't even lunchtime, but it felt like night, the sky had grown so dark. I never gave a thought to what Dougie might think if I didn't make it home. I'd been caught by weather or night many times in the past, going to ground at a friend's house if shelter was required, or sleeping rough in the down bag I carried on my treks. Never in weather this cold, but I don't think Dougie would have noted such a detail.

Look at that; as if he'd heard me think his name, Dougie's stirring. He'll have an awful crick in his neck; yes, there, he rubs it, looks around and starts guiltily to see me watching him. I suppose by some people's standards he is guilty. Yet I don't feel this myself, and not because I've been "unfaithful" too. "Unfaithful." The word makes my skin crawl with its country-western bittersweet self-pitying pain-glorifying stink. The truth is, he's more like a brother to me; he owes me nothing. It might even be the other way around, though I always had a part-time job and the rent from Mother's house to pay my way. I kept his house, cooked his meals, and did not fret him with complaints. Can I call that a fair trade? I think I must, as no means now remains to me to pay a debt.

But what is this? He's coming over to me, even turning the lamp so there's some light to see each other by. He looks a wreck.

"Are you okay, Dee?" he asks, using the bland nickname he invented to disguise the strangeness of "India" to his ears.

"In what sense?" I have to ask, though it's time to get past all that.

"No pain?"

"Not much. It doesn't matter."

"They can give you more . . ."

"No!" I say, quite sharply. "No," again, trying to sound calm and rational, so that he won't feel qualified to insist. I've already had some experience of how they take you over, no more a person but a Cancer Doll, a thing to which they apply strange remedies for its own good, regardless of the Me still resident.

Tit for tat. I did it to my mother, now I get it back. The words on the fluid bags have changed, but the essence remains the same. How she used to struggle, pulling the needles out until the visiting nurse was in despair. Like a wolf with its foot caught in a trap. Her mad eyes, so like the falcon's that day when it met my gaze as it swept past. Her nose, that had always been so broad and pudgy, was by then whittled down to bone. She tried to spit, but her mouth was dry and all she could do was make a little noise, *phtt, phtt.*

"I have to tell you . . ." Dougie's voice draws me back. "Dee? We need to talk."

"*I* don't need to talk," I say. "I don't need anything." Not quite the truth, but I have no time to try to explain my whole life to Dougie now. And I don't want to hear his remorse; I'm surprised at him. Confession and absolution for this poor lapsed Catholic? He'd do better to see the priest.

"No, I'm going to say it, Dee."

"One last time," I tell him, "don't call me Dee. Call me my real name. Then maybe I'll listen."

"Oh." He pauses, abashed. If he had a hat in his hands he would be holding it by the brim, rotating it round and round and round. "I never realized . . ."

"I said it once or twice."

"No, you . . ." He pauses, seeing, for once, the uselessness of that. "I guess I didn't hear you." Didn't listen, is more like it. "I'm sorry . . . India."

"You don't have to say. I know about Clarissa. It's all right."

"It isn't that."

I'm speechless. What can it mean? Does Dougie have a hidden depth, even one, that I've missed? It's all too likely, I'm afraid. I must make what amends I can. A vision of the rising falcon comes between us for a moment; I seem to hear the little bells. No, it's the spoon rattling on the tray the nurse brings in. Bad timing. "Go away," I say, surprising even myself with such rudeness. "Just for a minute?" Better. I will make a lady of myself yet. Something I never gave a damn about.

She goes. "Talk fast," I say. "Time is short." A little gallows humor to cheer us both up.

"I knew," he says, speaking slowly, seeming to choose his words, "about you and . . . that you went to bed with someone else. Not who. Just, you found someone."

I'm stunned again, twice in one night, and by a man whose capacity to surprise me I'd thought exhausted by . . . well, never mind by what. He goes on. "I don't blame you. That's what I want to say. I know I hurt you, with Clarissa and . . ." All those others, he doesn't say.

Too late; I hear it anyway. "I was wrong. I'm sorry. I never loved them, really. I was faithful to you, in my way. But you couldn't know that. I understand. You had your revenge. I forgive you."

Revenge! I'm so angry that I shout with laughter though it wears me out. Laugh until the tears come. "Oh, Dougie," I tell him, "what a lovely speech! You must have practiced all day." Where have I been keeping all this bitterness? Why can I not express it without an instant flood of remorse?

He doesn't know what to think. But never mind. There's not enough time left to make every wrong right. Besides, by the time the first sod falls on my coffin lid he will have redesigned this whole event into a heartfelt rapprochement. He will surely tell the next woman, with tears streaming down his face, that he forgave me as I lay here, almost on death's doorstep, and how we were both purified in that heartrending moment. He will move on, what else could he do? There was never any point in being cross with him.

It's this death business; it's put me off my stride. I used to be much kinder, or so I'd like to think. I didn't laugh at Mother the eighty-seven times she begged my pardon for ruining my life. I told her, honestly, that my life wasn't ruined at all. It never occurred to me to wonder whether that was really the comfort she wanted; it's only now, living through my own death, that I begin to see: she wanted forgiveness for her sin, not to have it whisked away, erased, denied. I should have said, "Yes, you did destroy my youth, turn my hopes to ashes, trample on my dreams. My life's an utter shambles, such was your power. But I love you anyway, and so I forgive you." If I'd said that, might she have died content? Sorry, Mother, I didn't understand.

As Dougie doesn't understand about the falconer. How Rhodri seemed to hear me in a way that made me hear myself, so that I rose, wing-beat by wing-beat, into another sort of being; how he made me fly.

And here's that nurse come back, hesitating just inside the door. "Just checking." There's a steaming cup on the tray. I wave my hand; a feeble gesture. Why won't they leave me be?

APRÈS-MIDI

OF THE SOUL

*R*hodri and I talked into the afternoon that day, laying the groundwork for our ephemeral house. Started with the particulars of our separate pasts, the ways that had led us to where we were. He spoke of his life as if it were an integrated whole, each part interlocked with every other, though he'd lived in five countries and half a dozen states. I spoke of mine as a series of accidents, though I've spent my whole life in a single town. But even as I said this, I saw that it was false, that every part of who I was and what I'd been had grown from what came before, that I had built each brand-new and separate (I thought) edifice of self from pieces I had salvaged from the one just lost.

I told him about the garden of native plants, the propagation techniques I'd figured out for myself because I couldn't find them in the books, the way I'd laid the lupine, the poppies, and the violets out in stars and swirls, ranged the creeping plants in a green rainbow, from dark glossy evergreens to the pale chartreuse of the soft-leaved meadow plant I'd never managed to identify. As I talked about it, I saw that it had been to me as the falcons were to him, a way to slip sideways between society's demands and the savage freedom that the caged heart keeps in secret.

When I mentioned how Jean Jones had urged me to try to get my findings published, he laughed, not even needing me to say that I had done it for the love of doing it, and because I would not let them tell me that I couldn't. Instructions would have robbed the whole enterprise of its point, and I cared not a whit whether others after me could do the same thing. I wanted no part of any plant-by-numbers schemes.

He told me about his struggle to find an alternative to his gas generator. He had to have a freezer to keep the quail frozen, and was quickly driven to admit that there was no way to run it but electricity. He could have used the same source of power to run lights indoors, but wanted fire in his house, wanted it semi-tamed at his command, to serve his needs. And to keep him keen and clear about the thing he fought.

He talked about threads running through his life: fire, flight, mountains, and solitude. I talked about the bakery, about the tribe's mask ceremonies that they'd never let an Anglo watch before I came, told him the tales of how I got the jeep and found the fox bone, both the same day. I didn't speak of death. A silence fell. I saw I'd offered only emptiness again.

"All right," I said. I sounded exasperated, even to myself, and restless where I'd been at ease for hours. I got up on the pretense of pouring the dregs of my coffee down the sink, and said what I had to with my back to him, looking out the window at the dark, cold day. "I'm going to die. I haven't told anyone else, but I guess I've got to tell you. I'd like to pretend it isn't happening, to go on as long as I can without admitting it to anyone. But there it is. Too big to ignore. Sorry about that. Sorry."

I heard him stand up, walk across the bare board floor to me. He turned me around, put his arms around me, held me like a mother, and I put my face against his chest and for the first time wept. Bawled. Choked and sobbed and even, God help me, bellowed. He stood there and let me, until I stopped. A long time, stroking my hair, rubbing my back.

Finally I seemed to be cried out. I pulled away. My head ached and my whole face felt swollen. I poured some water on my hands from the bottle by the sink and splashed my face.

"Tell me about it," he said.

"Not much to tell. Cancer. Like my mother, only faster; that's one good thing, at least. Hers took five years; horrible years. The doctor says I won't live through the spring."

I turned and looked at him for the first time since I'd said it. He was frowning slightly. "That's fast."

"It is now." I surprised myself. "Before, I didn't think it made much difference. Six months or sixty years, it didn't matter; just more of the same. Nothing to cry about."

THE HIGHER PLANE

I thought I'd ruined everything, falling apart like that. Pity was the last thing I wanted, from him or anyone else. I'd never been one to blub, hadn't done it but once since I was a kid, when my mother's heavy arm around my shoulders, her boozy breath in my face, had transformed my misery into in-turned rage, never again to give her such a chance. Poor baby! Not this child. I wanted more from her than that.

Rhodri and I went for a walk. He helped me on with the jacket again, wrapped a scarf around my neck, found gloves, ridiculously large on my hands. He brought along a lap robe and a rolled-up ground pad, tucking them both under one arm and taking my hand. I had to laugh. "You'd make some child a terrific mother," I told him as we started up the old logging road behind his house.

"Too bad about that," he replied, and I felt I had touched a sore place.

"Never married?"

He shook his head. "Never even thought about it."

"That shows great strength of character." I hadn't meant to let that face show, but he just smiled. I was so distracted by the feel of his hand enclosing mine, a sensation I hadn't experienced since childhood, that I scarcely noticed the elder saplings encroaching on the old dirt road, the wild thyme, the strawberry plants. None native to this spot; just more of mankind's clumsy bootprints, as infuriating as the scar of the road itself, and more pernicious. But when we turned up the first switchback and came face to face with the apple tree I stopped. "Just look at that! I ask you!"

"What?"

"Some idiot buried his apple core. Can't people ever just be in a place without changing it?"

"Even the bare fact of someone being there changes it. I've been looking for years for a spot in the world where no man or woman has ever stood before."

He tugged my hand, urging me past the apple tree and my annoyance. "I don't mean the top of K2, or Antarctica. Just somewhere so far off the beaten track that no one's ever been there. I don't think it exists anymore. We'd have to go back in time, maybe to when the land bridge first formed, before the Asian tribes came east. I'd like to go so far back that we could stand on top of this mountain and be absolutely, utterly alone."

I'd felt that way myself, could see it plainly as he spoke. "You'd feel as empty as a jug; the wind could blow right through you."

We had to scramble up the last steep feet, and then we were on the ridge, not much more than a yard wide, the whole other side of the mountain disclosed beneath our feet. Turning back the way we'd come, I could see the new roof of his house a hundred feet below, shingles in a pattern like dancing diamonds. Several miles past that, the China Flat. Hawks circled; it was too far to tell if any of them trailed leather straps with little bells attached.

He unrolled the ground pad and we sat side by side and stared out. "This is as close as we're going to get to un-explored territory now," he said. He put his arm around my shoulder and we looked awhile in silence. "Close enough." I knew he didn't mean the mountain.

"My great-grandmother used to hike." I'd forgotten this, but it all came back. "You might think because we've lived in this area for four generations, there'd be a load of lore, but it wasn't like that. Whatever Grandma knew about her mother, she didn't pass it on, or if she did, Mother was too gin-saturated already to soak it up. I think they probably didn't even attempt it; they didn't get along. But there was an old teacher, Miss Murphy, when I was a kid, who'd known Great-grandma after Great-grandpa died. Told me she used to hike; take a mule up into the hills and tie it by a stream and walk and walk. People thought she was peculiar."

"If she'd stood right here, she would have seen just what we're seeing, bar my cabin roof."

We'd fallen into a strange neutralness, so that his arm around my shoulders, though comforting, lit no spark. Yet I wasn't disappointed, there was no sag of spirits. Rather a mild elation, like the first whiff of laughing gas. "She was a sour old thing, by all accounts. I don't know why she went into the woods; maybe just to get away from people because she hated their guts. Maybe she came to kneel on cold stones and mortify her flesh. I've got a rosary she left, but they weren't Catholics." I hadn't made my point. "The thing is, I don't think she would see just what we're seeing even if she were standing right here this very minute."

"Don't you think you and I are seeing the same thing, then?"

"Probably not. Maybe the meadow where we lost the hawk. But to you it's also a place where lots of other stuff has happened. Where that same hawk came back every time but the last. And the roof of your house is a thing you made yourself. For me there's different thoughts. See over there." I pointed. "That highest peak but one on the left? I sat there with a pointy rock digging into my butt for an hour one afternoon, watching a bald eagle build a nest. Didn't dare leave until she was out of sight. And on the far side of the next mountain over, I found a clump of yellow violets in bloom a year ago May, and in September I went back and dug out a bit of the rootstock and it grew in my garden this summer. I could go on for hours; every place we can see from here has some memory attached. Layers of memory, each one building on the last. Sometimes I've thought of leaving Dougie and going someplace entirely different, just to see what a virgin landscape might be like."

"It doesn't work," he said. "You carry the old landscape along with you, and bits pop out and attach themselves to the new scenes. Before you know it, it's all right there again. You lay the shingles in that diamond pattern because that's the way you did it on the roof you helped your father lay when you were ten. The new meadow orients itself to lie the way the meadow in the Scottish Highlands lay the first time you ever flew a hawk. You can't get away from your own head." I could see it as he spoke, the young boy on the rooftree, earnestly pounding roofing nails beside his father. Sunlight.

"Lucky to have good things in it, then." I laid my own head briefly on his shoulder, then lifted it again to look at him. "So tell me, falconer, where are you now?"

"I'm here," he said. "I'm really here. I'm here at last."

ON THE

MOUNTAINTOP

*R*hodri had felt her confession of mortality like a knife through his chest. He'd heard about knife wounds: no pain at first, only a violent jolt and a sense of shock. He'd moved toward her almost involuntarily, turned her to him, held her for dear life, and as she began to cry the pain burst up, searing, so that he almost cried out. Before their lives had truly touched, the end was in sight. Until he felt their loss, he had not recognized his own hopes.

He held himself there for her like a man of stone, liquid lava burning within, but for her a warm firmness where she could rest and pour her grief. His arms ached with the restraint of his tenderness, the desire to tighten and press her to him forever. He would have to save his own grief for another time, too soon.

Finally she seemed emptied out, flaccid for the moment, like a beast that has just given birth. He took her out of doors, for some instinct to let her touch the earth and renew her strength. Up to the top of the mountain, where the wind could scour them both.

It seemed to work. Her voice grew stronger as she told him about the meanings hidden in their view. He could see her in her sturdy boots, tramping the hillsides to search out the wildwood's treasures. As her strength flowed back, his grief ebbed, so that when she turned to face him all that was left of its heat had pooled and concentrated just below his navel. She smiled that glorious smile that showed the origin of the lines bracketing her mouth, and he at last reached out and touched her face, the hesitant sweet curve of her upper lip. Her mouth relaxed, but the smile stayed in her eyes. Tracing the lip line down to one corner and cupping her cheek in the palm of his hand, he bent toward her very carefully until their lips met. He could feel her trembling.

The fire below his navel flared white-hot; it was no longer grief, though a hint of sorrow did remain. Laying her back on the ground pad, peeling their bodies to the day's cool air, he made love to her upon the mountaintop.

IN THE WHITE SKY

She was amazed at how quickly her numbness gave way to red desire. A slow delightful agony of want. Astonishing knife-keen pleasure of have. When he was in her she opened her eyes a moment, saw past his head a hawk circle round them once. Nothing had ever felt like this.

ALONE AT LAST

*E*ven lying here, hours from death, I still tingle when I think about it. And burn with anger and regret, that we didn't meet years ago, when there was still time. Back in 1978, when Mother was at her worst, Rhodri was looking for another job. He had grown tired of flying air survey on loan to the UAE, though the money was fantastic, and untaxed. He'd saved enough to buy his house, set up his mews. Was looking for a job back in the Americas. There'd been an offer in California then, up near Mount Lassen, but he'd turned it down in favor of something in South Dakota, geographically more suitable for hawks.

It's the closest he ever got to intersecting my orbit; not so very close; Mount Lassen's several hundred miles north. We combed our pasts, searching for ways we might have met before. I went down to LA once with Dougie, soon after we were married, to go to Disneyland. Rhodri's

never been near the place. He was at Yosemite once, to help put out a big fire there in the early eighties. I wasn't close. We read some of the same magazines: the *Geographic, Outdoor Life,* but neither ever wrote to the editor. Once about ten years ago I'd entered a contest where ten first prizes were offered: trips to Alaska on a new cruise ship. He'd seen the same promotion, but never entered it.

Our attempts to find a way we might have met grew more and more fanciful. What if I'd taken a driving trip, from White Creek to Ann Arbor, and what if at the same time he had decided to trek from Rapid City to Memphis? And what if our cars had both broken down in Kansas City, where our paths would cross, and we'd gone for repairs to the same garage on the same day? We might have had years together, if only we hadn't been so far apart.

What if I'd left Dougie in the summer of '85, when I was so close to it?

THIS WAY OUT

*I*t's hard to remember how I used to feel about Dougie, how I used to be. When I told Jean Jones, the only friend I had in town after five years closed in that house with Mother, that Dougie had asked me to marry him, she said, "About time you had some happiness." Looking back on that I notice it didn't strike me as funny at the time.

I know that's not much evidence, but it seems better than the purely negative fact that when I found out about him and Prinny Dufour, it hurt.

First of all, it hurt because Prinny didn't have one thing about her I could envy. She was and still is a plain, worn-out-looking woman, too thin, too hoarse, and wearing too much makeup. She's older than I am, and has made a twenty-year career out of pulling beers at the local bars, moving from one to the next each time she has a fight with the boss. She works her way around the circuit, only three bars in town, about every five years, and by the time she gets back where she started, there's usually new management. There've been a lot of optimists come to White Creek, looking for the gold in them thar hills and cutting their losses when the supply of gainfully employed drunks proves too meager to make them rich.

It wasn't that she was sleeping with Dougie and the whole town knew it. All right, I did mind that, but that wasn't the worst of it. The worst was the way I found out: she staged a confrontation. In the bakery, while I was at work. All that tawdry pathetic bullshit: "Let him go, I love him and you don't" (bring on the violins), in front of Reba and Earl; it was a wonder they didn't fire me. I couldn't make up my mind whether to reach for the gun Earl kept under the cash register, or to go for a chocolate cream pie and hit her square in the face, so I just stood there gaping at her, to my lasting regret. I ought to have put that on my last-chance list: throw a chocolate pie at Prinny Dufour. Strange I didn't think of it.

Dougie apologized very nicely, actually got down on his knees (in the kitchen, not a public place) and promised that it had all been "a terrible mistake," that he had "lost his mind," it was "just physical" and "really you I love," and "would never happen again." And I stood there looking down at the top of his head (he was crying noisily into the hem of my skirt) and realized that I no longer loved him, I could hardly remember that I ever had, and I was flooded with relief. I wonder why on earth I was wearing a skirt?

When I told Jean about this, she asked, "What are you going to do?" and for a moment I couldn't think what she meant.

"You mean, leave him?" It was like a revelation. I pictured myself in a tailored suit, gray wool, maybe, with a discrete vertical chalk stripe, striding along a city sidewalk with a briefcase and a breezy look.

Doing what? For months that question tortured me the way "why" does now. On the one hand I had my mother's house, rented and bringing in a little income. I could sell it, but I wouldn't get much. Who's going to buy a house built in 1892, wired for electricity in 1908 and again in 1952, and plumbed in 1935 and left to rust? The floors sagged, the stairs creaked, none of the windows fit. I was lucky to get two hundred a month for it from Billy Boseman, whose mother had finally thrown him and his twenty cats into the street when he forgot her sixty-fifth birthday.

On the other hand, I had no work experience. Nobody carries a briefcase to a job piping frosting roses on birthday cakes. I'd heard about those city rents; more than I made in three months in White Creek, so that even if wages were higher there (they'd have to be, wouldn't they?), and I worked full-time, even then there wouldn't be enough.

Meanwhile Dougie was being extremely sweet. Flowers. Candy. Not original, but at least he was trying.

Every night he came home early, undressed in the bathroom, put his own dirty clothes into the laundry hamper (instead of strewing them on the floor) and asked politely if I was in the mood. And though I never was, I sometimes said yes, because it didn't matter much and seemed to please him so. He said things like "I know you can't forgive me right away, but I'm going to show you . . ." Never exactly saying what.

"Go on, girl," Jean kept urging me. "Get out while you can. You'll find something; just go!" But I held back. Prinny was giving me the evil eye every time we met, but Dougie hadn't been near her since the shoot-out at the bakery, I knew that. It was tempting to walk out, leave him to her with the knowledge that she was second choice. Though this thought did occupy my mind sometimes, deep down it didn't move me much. I looked around my house and found it good. More than good; it was my place. The kitchen cabinets I'd refaced myself with fumed oak; the garden of healthy native plants in formal beds, a cross between *Wild Kingdom* and Versailles; my mountain walks.

My mother's house. Could I part with that? Four generations, mother to daughter, each one before me dying in the front bedroom. I've thought of making them take me there to die myself, but what would become of Billy and the cats?

I still haven't reached the heart of it. Why did I stay? I'm a mystery to myself. All I can remember is that the idea of leaving gradually faded away. I spent more and

more time in the garden and on walks, got interested in
the medicinal uses of the plants, and forced my acquain-
tance on Josephine Red Smoke, the tribal matriarch who
lived above the beauty parlor and always seemed to have
three or four infants "staying" with her. She taught me the
native names of the plants, what they were for. She let me
hold the babies. She sold me the jeep and gave me my
name: Fox Bone Woman. I felt new and strong, complete
either without the marriage or with it, no matter what
form it took. And when Dougie stopped apologizing and
began again to stay out late, I noticed and said nothing,
and my life was set.

Now it seems that if I'd left, I might have had a
chance. Some accident surely would have drawn me to
North Carolina, to meet Rhodri there. Or if not there, a
few years later I might have gone to Idaho. Fate might
have washed me up anywhere, if only I'd had the sense to
let go of the rock I was clinging to. If only I'd believed
there was a Fate.

WITH THIS RING

We finally came down off the mountain and by then it was midafternoon. Some choices had to be made. Like: what next? Both of us knew that the only thing for it was to have me stay with him. In a town the size of White Creek you can't say "hi" to a stranger in the street without having to explain it three thousand times before breakfast the next day. But the minute you get past that bend in Main Street, out onto the Arbuckle Road, you just about disappear.

Rhodri brewed up another round of coffee to warm me for my trip back, where I'd pick up what I needed for a stay of some sort. We weren't being too specific. We were like Wendy and John and Michael after Peter Pan has taught them to fly; we'd stopped thinking and were just doing it.

I sat in that armchair by the fire, took off my ring, and looked at it. Rhodri saw it in my hand when he brought the coffee. His eyebrows rose, but he didn't say anything. "I don't know what to do with it," I said.

"It's a problem," he agreed. I was so glad he hadn't said "throw it out," or pretended not to understand.

"I don't even know what it is," I said. "Symbol of a promise I never should have made in the first place, and broke today without a moment of regret."

He kissed me and handed me my coffee. "What's he like?"

"Oh, lord. Another impossible question. Where do I start?"

"I shouldn't have asked. It's not the right question."

"I guess not. All I can say is, if he found out, I don't think he'd be hurt." It wasn't much, but even at that, it was more compunction than I'd felt about Dougie for many a long year; strange time to discover these feelings in myself.

I stuck the ring in my pants pocket and drank my coffee, and that was the end of that.

RHODRI'S ARGUMENT

*H*e figured people would have to know about them at some point. He could rent a hospital bed down in Vinton, but sooner or later nurses would be required, and anyway her husband would have to be told. She'd been on the mountain for ten days now without her absence from home exciting any comment, but six months or more would surely be a different story.

"What are you thinking?" she asked him.

"Just trying to figure whether I'll need a bigger generator."

"What for?"

"So you can have one of those electric hospital beds that goes up and down when you push the button."

"Uh-oh," she said, and his gut lurched.

She wasn't going to stay. Didn't want him to see

her fall apart. It wasn't exactly a quarrel, but definitely an argument. "You think I'd turn squeamish on
you?"

"It isn't that."

"Nothing's going to change me. You could turn into
a snail and I'd love you just the same. We've got so little
time as it is; don't make it less."

They'd been in their favorite spot—in front of the
fire, where they'd constructed a sort of nest out of their
sleeping bags. She touched his face; he could never resist
that look, the steady gaze that saw into his soul. "It could
never be less."

"You know I'll do whatever you want. It doesn't matter; only let me be with you."

"Oh, heart, I want that too. Forever, if there is such
a thing."

"How not?" he asked. "Something like this can't melt
into the void. We're taking huge pieces of the power of
the universe and forging them into a bond between us
and a ward around us that will never come apart. Don't
you feel that?"

"I feel it, but . . ."

"Don't say 'but.' You've got to believe it; that's an es-
sential part. My mother used to say people find what they
expect after death; we used to pity all those poor Calvin-
ists, sitting on hot coals forever because it's what they
imagined."

"Where's your mother, then?"

He laughed. "She had a vision of heaven as a huge library; she's up there, still writing away."

"And you?"

"I'll fly. With you. That's all I want."

It made him fearful, the way she said, "I hope." She didn't believe it yet.

TWENTY-FOUR DAYS,
FOUR HOURS, AND
FIFTEEN MINUTES

*I*t's no wonder Dougie figured it out. I was hardly home a minute while my time with Rhodri lasted. The only reason I didn't suspect that he suspected must have been that, after the ring question, I slipped completely into my new life. Nothing else existed; just Rhodri, the hawks, and the mountaintop.

I did go home late that first afternoon, but didn't stay the night. Stuck the ring in the back of the drawer where I keep old sweaters too good to throw away, and left a note saying I was off and not to worry. I didn't like writing it, but I put it as a PS. "I'll be back." I didn't bother to explain. Maybe I subconsciously figured that he'd think I was out exploring again; I'd done it enough times before, sometimes as long as ten days. Mostly I didn't care. I grabbed clothes, toothbrush, whatever. I was in such a hurry to get back I could hardly concentrate. Took time for a shower, since hot water was a pump-and-stove thing

at Rhodri's place, but forgot nightgowns, and underwear. Forgot my slippers, too, which I sorely missed.

If Rhodri hadn't had to go down to Lanark to the airfield every weekday afternoon to work, we might have died of love. I spent the time while he was gone playing house, wearing my own jeans and his big shirts and socks, washing the windows, reading his falconry books, cooking dinners for us both. What would have been deadly chores in any other place were fairy-tale tasks; I mastered the woodstove, the balky pump, the flue's persnickety demands.

I often slept, and pretended it was normal to need a four-hour nap after a good night's rest. Pretended it was because of the waking up to make love, the sleepy urge sometimes coupling us before we were fully conscious. Each time he reached for me, my flame leapt up to meet him; each time I reached for him he rose to readiness in a rush of heartbeats, like a bird taking the air.

I managed to hide my growing weakness with those naps. On the days he was off duty it was harder, sometimes a real struggle to stay bright, and those nights I might have been slower to awaken to his slumberous caress. We even slept all night the last two Sunday nights. At least, I never woke up.

He had only a small mirror, propped above the kitchen sink, where he shaved each morning. I saw my face as I washed it, and wished I had something to hide the circles that appeared beneath my eyes. I felt my ribs growing more prominent. In the firelight one night

Rhodri traced them with his finger. "You're not eating enough."

"Shhh," I said. "None of that talk. I haven't changed; I'm never going to change. Don't even think it." I knew it was useless, but wanted to stave it off as long as I could. Never to let him see me fading, let alone the way Mother got. I remembered that with knifelike clarity: the bedsores and stinking breath, the anger she felt at her own incontinence and vented on me while I cleaned her up. If she'd been crazy before, she became in the last days almost a demon, forgetting who I was and screaming in my face. No, I had no plan to make him go through that.

We flew the falcons together every day, the five of them. Sir Kay never came back. He had a smaller bird, a male called Gawain, cross between a merlin and a goshawk, that he called mine. I flew all the birds at different times. The shortwings were funny, their mad suspicious eyes and the way they'd jump off the rabbit-skin lure to snatch at a much smaller piece of a dead chick. "Not very bright," Rhodri remarked. "Every falconer knows a bird in the hand is worth two in the bush; we made up that saying ourselves. But the birds never seem to figure it out."

CONFESSIONAL

One night as we lay in the dark together after our bodies' fire had been satisfied, he said, "There is one thing I haven't told you yet. Something I've never told a soul."

There was a tone in his voice I hadn't heard before. I was flooded with panic, and tried to make a joke. "Don't tell me you were Jack the Ripper in a former life."

"Not quite as grim as that. I have a daughter."

A picture of Dougie's worried face and a hospital ceiling flashed in my mind as I paused, searching for the way to answer this. "I'm jealous."

He laughed. Not a merry laugh. "It's not like that."

He hadn't even known about her birth. Visiting in Toronto after his stint in South Dakota, he'd been having lunch with some old family friends when this woman dropped by. Someone he'd slept with once, casually, on a visit to the city five years before, between his time in the Emirates and taking up the job he'd then just left. She had her daughter with her, a girl who'd recently turned four. He couldn't take his eyes off her, she looked so much like his mother.

When the woman left, he made a clumsy excuse and went with her. Janet, her name was. He didn't know what to say; the child was right there, Gillie, her big solemn eyes watching him with what he felt as a far from casual curiosity. "We've got to talk."

"There's nothing to talk about."

"You don't want me to say it all right now, do you?"

"I thought you were more of a gentleman than that," she had said. He didn't care what she thought.

She dropped the child at a friend's house, took Rhodri to a little park nearby. "Don't get ideas," she'd said. "I've been married to Paul since she was a year old. She thinks he's her father. There's no place for you in this picture."

He'd been too furious to speak, clenched his hands to hide their trembling, and lest he take this woman by the throat and change the course of both their lives. Even talking about it ten years later, in my arms, I could feel him struggling with the pain; his whole body seemed to vibrate with it. "It was like she'd robbed me, raped me in cold blood."

She'd been perceptive enough to see his rage. "It wasn't on purpose, Rhodri. I'm the one that should be angry. I'm the one that got knocked up and had to deal with the consequences. You can't blame me for making a life for us."

He wanted to tell her she could have written and

told him, he would have come back, married her, anything. He didn't say it, didn't know whether he would
have or not. They'd hardly known each other their one
night, hardly knew each other now. "Don't upset the ap-
plecart," Janet had begged. "Try to imagine you've do-
nated sperm to a sperm bank or something. She has a
good life, two parents who love her, security, everything a
child needs. Knowing about you could only mess her up."

He knew she was right. He left Toronto for the last
time, dropped the friends they had in common. The new
job was challenging and there was a new sort of hawk to
fly, the shortwings they were breeding in Mexico.

He couldn't stop thinking about Gillie, how when
she met his eyes for a moment it was like seeing his mother
look at him from the child's face. He hired a private inves-
tigator to make sure she was all right, to send him a picture
once a year. From his lonely distance, he'd watched her
grow more and more like the grandmother she would
never know about. She was fourteen now, getting to the
difficult part; he worried. "I've thought about writing her
a letter, something she'd get if she looked, but not other-
wise. But I don't know what I'd say." He didn't cry. I held
him until his limbs relaxed. A daughter. Age fourteen.

It was a long time before I went to sleep. All the old
questions were clamoring in my head. Why had I stayed?
How could I have left? Was this revelation another proof
that the forces of the world had meant us to be together,
or just another damn coincidence? I saw the shape, but
not yet what it meant.

NIGHT AND DAY

*T*hey seem to be running some kind of Midnight Olympics around here. Every time I close my eyes, there's that nurse to take my temperature, to turn me so I don't get bedsores, to plump my pillows. I don't want my pillows plumped. I want to be left alone. Dougie is back in his armchair, snoring again. I suppose our little talk was cathartic for him. I always thought if I left him he'd fall apart, but here I go, and I suppose he'll be all right. He'll find someone else to keep track of his glasses and his crossword puzzles, and to cook him low-fat food so his little pot doesn't turn into a big pot. Clarissa, or this nurse, or someone else. It beats me how such a befuddled soul can attract so much loving assistance. He's got the sympathy of every female in town; they all know I'm half-crazy and neglect him. They'll have to put me in a double-wide grave so there'll be enough room for all the women who want to dance on it.

If, if, if. If I'd sold my mother's house, instead of renting it out all these years, I could have gone. Maybe I would have gone to Toronto, been the one he slept with that night. Round and round. Would he have loved the girl I was then? It seems to me looking back that I had no character at twenty-three. I was like yesterday's balloon, most of my buoyancy gone, just enough left to drift along near the ground. Couldn't see any way to go back and pick up the path I'd planned to take five years before, couldn't see any way to go forward, couldn't seem to move at all, of my own volition.

I said something like that to Jean once, and she said it was grief, post-traumatic shock, a delayed reaction. I think it was more the bewilderment of the maggot when you remove its protecting rock. Sunlight! Wait! I'm not ready to move to the next instar yet! The exposed larvae squirm about, trying blindly to nuzzle their way back to the dark. I married Dougie, lost my chance to find Rhodri while there was still time. Still, as Dougie is fond of saying (his only philosophical comment), we'll never know what would have happened if what did happen hadn't happened.

OUTWARD BOUND

*R*hodri and I did all the things on my list: the balloon ride, the visit to the ocean, the river raft. We searched for a thunder egg down in the desert, half a day's drive away, but we found only agate and a small piece of polished rose quartz that some tourist had probably dropped. We stayed in the desert overnight, awake and looking at the zillion stars. He said the vault of heaven was like a dome of glass over one of those Christmas scenes you shake, with stars instead of snow, and we were safe inside it and would endure forever.

We found a flat place amid the scrubby madrona and dusty sage, made a circle of stones, and built a fire. There wasn't a human sound except our voices. Hardly a sound at all, just the crackling of the fire. We'd been picking up bits of dead mesquite all day, between looking for round rocks that weren't as heavy as they should have been. Either the rock hounds had been here before us and picked

the place clean, or we were in the wrong place to begin with. Not a geode could we find. I hadn't really expected that we would. It was enough to be there, with him. Especially in the firelight.

I can see his face; he was looking at the flames and I was looking at him, how the firelight gilded his profile. The sparks flew up. "What do you think we would have fought about?" I asked.

He looked at me and smiled and shook his head. "Do people always fight?"

"If they care," I said, expressing an opinion I'd never been conscious of. "Only I couldn't bear it if you were angry with me."

He poked the ground between his feet with the stick he'd been using to stir the fire. "You might get upset about how much time I have to spend with the birds. Bored, maybe, if I talked about them too much."

"Never; they're so much a part of you. But you might get tired of having me tag along? Maybe I'd get in your way, or be clumsy, mess up somehow."

"Should we have a fight now?" he asked, smiling as if he were almost daring me to say yes. I might have laughed, only I realized he'd caught me.

"I'd like to, in a way."

He nodded.

"Only I don't think I can," I said.

"Maybe we could just pretend we'd fought, skip ahead to the making up?" He threw the stick into the fire and moved closer to me, facing me. "I didn't mean it," he said. "I'm sorry." His eyes were full of sorrow, too; I could hardly breathe.

"It doesn't matter," I said, whispered, hearing the fire crackle, hearing the stars sigh. "It's all right." I kissed him, and he picked me up and carried me to our sleeping bags. It was like a dream to feel so loved, so wanted, so complete.

It was cold enough for forever; we huddled together all night, got up at dawn and drank gallons of coffee to get warm, then had to pee behind every clump of mesquite for miles. As we flew Morgaine in the early desert light, a wild hawk appeared, and the two of them did a kind of dance, circling each other in elaborate loops until it made me dizzy to watch. Rhodri seemed unconcerned, and sure enough, the wild hawk broke off and went its way, and Morgaine came to his whistle. The early morning cold brought tears to my eyes.

That was the first expedition, when I still had some strength. Luckily the rest were easier.

Nothing to do in a balloon but gawk, as you sail above the valley's agribusiness with its clean-ruled quilt of fields, a patchwork of food and safety and separateness.

Nothing to do in a raft but lie back and enjoy the floating ride, horizon narrowed to the river's edge, ever-changing and ever the same.

And when it came to looking at the ocean, that was the least effort of all; I never even got out of the truck. There was no temptation, in November, to actually touch that water. We drove north awhile, on a road that over-

looked the beach. Empty. I couldn't believe the vastness; it seemed bigger than the sky. I was sorry we hadn't brought the birds on that trip; what would they have made of it?

Back home by late afternoon, I fell asleep as Rhodri lit the fire, and woke to find him looking at me with worry written large upon his face. "All that fresh air," I lied, and was careful after that. Rested when he wasn't looking. Ate as much as I could. By the third week I was sleeping almost every minute he wasn't there. In his presence, I managed to hide the growing pain, though sometimes in bed at night, as we were falling into sleep, my legs would twitch and jerk. Then came the day, thank God it happened while he was at work, I started to trek across the room from chair to sink and found myself suddenly on the floor, sitting in a pool of my own urine. The spell passed, and I got it all cleaned up and out of sight before he came home, but not out of mind. Our time was nearly up.

We lay in front of the fire that night and I traced the outline of his face, a memory exercise. He leaned on one elbow and looked down at me, and the orange glow of the flames glinted gold in his eyebrows, yellowed the silver threads in his fox-brown hair. I drew the lines on his forehead with my fingernail, traced his crow's-feet and his smile lines, the crease across his chin. He could tell something was up; he didn't ask. "I'm going tomorrow," I said.

"No," he said. "Stay here. Let me take care of you.

How can I not be there? How can I not be the one who holds your hand, brings your food, sits with you?"

"There's more to it than that."

He knew what I meant; I'd spoken of my mother's death, how I didn't want him to remember me like that, wasted and witless, how I didn't want to see him seeing me like that.

"A month, a year, a lifetime, what's the difference? Love is whole. We've had it all already." I said it, but I don't know if I believed it myself. "All I have left is to be able to remember us like this. I don't want you pitying me, and you wouldn't be able to help it."

He bent over me and gathered me to him, held me right up into his heart, so hard I knew he was memorizing too, and I held him too, with as much strength as I had. I felt his shoulders under my hands, the strong thick blades well muscled, where wings would be attached. I felt him rise with desire and my own flame burned up to meet him, and the fire inside us and outside us seemed all one burning light that might lift us straight to heaven on the tower of joy and anguish in our hearts.

PARTING

He helped me gather up my stuff. I put on the white pants and white shirt I'd been wearing the first morning I came up, but left the fox's vertebra behind, hidden under his pillow for him to find. We stood beside the jeep for a long time, silent. The birds in their mews clamored, for once ignored but urging me on my way. "Think of me as dead already," I said. "Don't picture the rest of it. Promise."

"I promise."

He helped me into the jeep, and followed in his truck all the way down the Oneida Road, down the paved potholed Vreeland Road, down the Arbuckle Road, just to the edge of town. Stopped by the Baptist Church and watched me out of sight, as I watched him, tiny in the rearview mirror that said across his chest "objects in mirror are closer than they look," until the turn of Main Street broke the thread. Jean tells me she saw me and waved and shouted from the sidewalk, asking where I'd been. I don't remember that, or answering "mountaintops," or driving past the school, up the slope of the driveway, into the parking place where the jeep had sat in its off-duty hours for the past ten years. Don't remember a thing until I walked into the kitchen and there was Dougie, wearing an apron and God alone knows where he got *that,* and I said, "I'm home." He dropped one of the good plates.

THE END

So what does it mean? I've been over it dozens of times as my life ebbs away. Two sides to every coin: heads, we found each other in spite of everything; tails, it was too late. "Too late for what?" he asked me once. Too late for everything: for a lifetime of sharing, for quarrels and making up, for really knowing each other. Yes, that's the real ache. Three weeks of constant talk is just a start, where things are supposed to begin. Even skipping as much small talk as we could, there are vast tundras still untracked. I don't know what color his mother's eyes were, or whether he was ever stung by a wasp. I don't know whether he went to his senior prom or whether he likes daffodils or not. I never got to fly in an airplane with him, or see him with other people. Never found out what it was he wanted to put into that letter to Gillie he had yet to write. Probably never did write. It seems now that it was all about me, as if we'd agreed it was no use filling my head with him, when it would soon go blank. So instead he listened, and in the end I told him not everything, but as much as I could fit. Is that some kind of immortality? Short-term life extension, at least. It would have been good to die and wake up in his skull, I think. His thoughts seemed as clear and sharp as snowmelt.

"Why do you love me?" I asked him once.

"I don't know," he answered immediately. "Other women have pleased me, made me laugh, engaged my interest for a week or two, but there was always some kind of distance; I never really felt them. Emotionally, touching them was like touching a hologram. You I can feel even when you're not in sight. Feel you right down to the heart."

My thoughts are going in circles, I know. I've grown too weak to straighten them out. In a while it will be dawn; another dreary dawn. Dougie will get up, go and shave. The nurse will come and clean me up. And still no answer, not a hint. And time is running out.

WIDER VIEW

*O*nly consider how everything he touched was changed. My life in total and in many parts. A sort of laying on of hands; perhaps I even expected that his magic would penetrate not just my female parts but my whole body, and bring about spontaneous remission of the crab crawling toward my backbone. Yet in a sense he did change even that, from "death, a trifle premature" to "Glorious Life, Cut Short."

Example: As we drifted down the American River in our boat of air and rubber, I told him about Sitting on the Rock. There's a small stream that runs through White Creek, turning tame and pastoral in the little level space occupied by the town. This stream runs behind the backyard of my mother's house, and in the middle of it a flat rock rises a couple of feet above the normal water level. Which is only about ten inches.

In times of trouble I would use that spot as my secret refuge, hardly secret, as there was no place more visible for a country mile. But the stream was broad, though shallow, and my mother had an aversion to wetting her feet (or any other part except her throat), and so when crisis burst upon the house, I made my escape to where she could or would not go. I don't know why this was so effective. She would stand on the bank, ten feet from where I perched, and tell me what she thought in words both loud and rude. She never had offered me any physical violence, so it was not fear of that that made me feel safer out of her reach. The one time she did risk pneumonia and plunge into the stream to shout from closer up, she neglected to take her shoes off, and the slippery leather soles gave her no foothold on the river stones. She fell, was doused, and as I told the story to Rhodri I remembered the rest: she'd laughed. All her crossness had just vanished; she'd sat there in the water and splashed some toward me, actually giggling. And now I recall that sometimes she could be like that. Yes. Playing with me like an overexcited child, wild and clever and out of control. Not just that day but other times as well. A mashed-potato-throwing "fight" one night at dinner. A pan of homemade bubble stuff in the backyard and her chasing the bubbles with a carving knife. Times I forget as often as I remember them, and when they do come back I'm puzzled all over again at their repeated loss. I'm filled with a kind of pleasure/pain that bewilders me. It made me glad Rhodri was there.

I told the story to him with a lot of detail, the fuzz of

the cottonwood trees sticking to her wet dress, the way she'd scared the fish, the slotted spoon she'd been carrying. I laughed, thinking of how her shoes had oozed water in a gush when she stepped out onto the stream's bank.

Rhodri said, "There, you see, you do believe in something. Some kind of magic made that place safe for you." And as soon as he said it, it was as if the light had changed in my memory, as if I were looking at myself upon that rock at a different time of day, or from a different spot along the bank, and I saw that it was true, I had gone there because the rock was sacred to me in some way, and gave me strength. Its power had turned my mad mother into a playmate for me, the elusive key suddenly found at just the right moment, even if in the end it vanished and she was changed back.

FATE MISSES

*H*ere's the bottom line at last: The shape of his desire was me, the shape of mine was him. If nature abhors a vacuum, how was it we weren't drawn together like two magnets? The only answer is, there is no Fate. No guardian angels watching, no benign deity who cares about our souls, not even a perfect clock set going and abandoned by the Celestial Clockmaker. Nothing but blind happenstance. Think how many poor souls that leave without their perfect mates, their ideal jobs, even the well-suited children they might have had in an orderly universe. We're all just out there bouncing in a vacuum, using our feeble will to turn this way or that, and only a lucky few happen to bounce into the place or person that will make their lives complete.

I said that to the falconer and he laughed at the picture of us as tiny homunculi flying through life like pop-

corn in a popper, but disputed my conclusion. "After all," he always ended his argument, "we did find each other at last." Too late, that was my point. But it was difficult to maintain it while his mouth burnished my skin until it felt as hot as a live coal. Passion's a kind of magic, I'll admit, but still no sort of argument.

THE LONG-AWAITED

DAWN

he birds outside the window are waking up. Dougie is not; he's snoring again, his head thrown back. He looks very uncomfortable. This is the worst time of day, the gray of dawn which ought to mean hope and life, but somehow always smells of despair. Mother waking up sober, with a groan, out of cigarettes. My sheets are damp with sweat, and this is the coldest time of day as well. I'll catch my death. Ha ha.

It was this time of day I woke in the hospital and realized my hopes of a child were sunk. The five-month baby who took only a few breaths and then expired. The problem that had expelled her prematurely. All in letters of fire against the gray sky of dawn. Dougie was there, asleep. He's good at sickbeds, I have to give him that. He woke up and saw my silent tears, pouring from the corners of my eyes, down over my temples and into my ears. He got tissues and blotted most of them away, leaving lit-

tle cold puddles in the hard-to-reach places. He held my hand and didn't speak. His eyes were wet, too. Maybe it was that, those unshed tears at dawn, that kept me with him all these years.

That should have been Rhodri's child. Same year, three thousand miles apart. Mine was a girl, too, they said.

I try to lift my head and find I can't. It won't be long now, I think. There's no pain at present, but my thoughts are extra clear, or maybe I'm so doped up I only think they're clear. My Occam's razor extra sharp. I riffle through the deck of memories once again, comparing shapes. Falcon wing, angel wing, airplane wing; longbow and perch; the crazy quilt of fields seen from the sky; the curve of the birds' flight and the curve of Rhodri's shoulder under my fingers. The lines on a map, on a globe, Rhodri's flights. My own dot, made of much traveling back and forth in the same small space; if I were an electron, I'd be hot.

There, the sun's coming up. Just the pinpoint gleam of it at the horizon, quickly leaping to a sliver, an arc. And someone knocking on the door, and Dougie waking up.

The nurse comes, something in her hand. "Is she awake? Oh, good. Someone brought a card." She puts it in my hand; I can barely lift it. "India," it says on the outside, Rhodri's handwriting.

"Who?" I ask. "Who brought this?"

"Dan Jones." Jean's husband, Forest Service boss. "He's been up to that fellow's house, the one who died? To see about some parakeets, but they were gone. He found this, so he brought it along as soon as he could . . ." Before I die, she meant.

I'm so weak I can barely open the envelope; my fingers fumble and shake, not just from feebleness. Inside is a picture of Morgaine on my hand. I remember the day he took it, almost the last day, though he didn't know it. He'd bought one of those disposable cameras, took a whole roll of me and the birds. When he'd moved up close to get this shot, Morgaine had objected to his approach, his strange crouch as he leaned forward to snap it; her wings were spread, her bright eye fearsomely intent. That's all the picture shows; the bird and the gloved hand beneath. On the back it says, "I'll be waiting."

"I didn't know you knew the pilot," Dougie says.

"Did you not?" The envelope slips off the edge of the bed, but I hold the picture to my heart. It's almost too much to grasp. I know the answer already, but move toward it step by step. No birds, therefore he let them go. He put this message out where I would surely get it. Therefore, he knew that he was going to die. Therefore . . . he died on purpose. To make the message true; to be there, because he knew there is a "there," waiting for me. I can't take it in, though in a sense I already have. Again he's changed the whole of my life, past and present, up, down and sideways, at a stroke. Rewritten history.

I'm stunned by the strength of his belief. It seems to grasp me in sinewy arms from the picture in my hand, shouting that there *is* a pattern, a meaning, and a truth. A

place beyond this one, where we'll fly together. And how can I doubt it now, when he knew it well enough to shed his life? It would be like doubting the falcon's flight, the fire's warmth, the bond between us.

In the blaze of this new knowledge, I see something else; that I, who always thought I was so strong, have been in fact a coward, weak. All my life. Afraid to trust, afraid to try, afraid to risk. Barricaded in my room for fear of fear itself. Crippled by doubt. But now it's not too late. Finally, it's not too late. I *can* take up my life and walk. Could have done it any time.

I see the picture slip out of my fingers as I rise. The nurse reaches for my wrist, looking alarmed; I really don't know why. I stretch my wings, they're wide and tingle. I try an experimental wave to get the feel of them; then with one powerful stroke I'm lifted to the sky, and there he is, just as he promised. See how he shines! Smiling, he reaches out to take my hand. A voice somewhere below me says, "My god, she's gone," and as I swoop into his arms I think, "They've got it wrong again. I'm really here, I'm here, I'm here at last!"

ABOUT THE AUTHOR

ELAINE CLARK MCCARTHY began writing at the age of nine, and through the years has written poems, screenplays, plays, and short stories. *The Falconer* is her first novel.

ABOUT THE TYPE

This book was set in Berling. Designed in 1951 by Karl Erik Forsberg for the Typefoundry Berlingska Stilgjuteri AB in Lund, Sweden, it was released the same year in foundry type by H. Berthold AG. A classic oldface design, its generous proportions and inclined serifs make it highly legible.